"Do you know what you are and why you're here, Roger?"

He considered the questions for a moment. He ran them through his memory, but came up empty. "No," he said.

Dr. Naughton nodded. "Roger, you are an android. Do you know what an android is?"

Roger answered: "A robot constructed to look and act like a human being."

"Right." Dr. Naughton smiled.

"Here," said the female. She held a mirror in her hand. "Take this and look at yourself."

Roger saw a human face gazing back at him from the mirror. He looked fully human. "I am an Adam unit?"

"No!" Dr. Naughton looked startled. "The Adam . . . *Adam* is a human child. Do you understand the difference?"

"Of course," Roger answered. "He is real, while I am artificial."

"That's right," said Dr. Naughton, greatly relieved.

The Outer Limits™

A whole new dimension in adventure . . .

#1 The Zanti Misfits
#2 The Choice
#3 The Time Shifter
#4 The Lost
#5 The Invaders
#6 The Innocent
#7 The Vanished
#8 The Nightmare

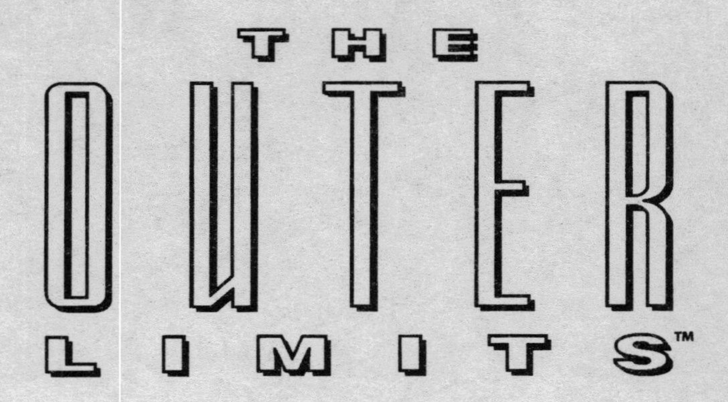

BEWARE THE METAL CHILDREN

JOHN PEEL

Tor Kids!

A TOM DOHERTY ASSOCIATES BOOK
NEW YORK

NOTE: If you purchased this book without a cover you should be aware that this book is stolen property. It was reported as "unsold and destroyed" to the publisher, and neither the author nor the publisher has received any payment for this "stripped book."

This is a work of fiction. All the characters and events portrayed in this book are either products of the author's imagination or are used fictitiously.

THE OUTER LIMITS #9: BEWARE THE METAL CHILDREN

A Tor Book
Published by Tom Doherty Associates, Inc.
175 Fifth Avenue
New York, NY 10010

Tor® is a registered trademark of Tom Doherty Associates, Inc.

ISBN: 0-812-57566-0

First edition: February 1999

Printed in the United States of America

0 9 8 7 6 5 4 3 2 1

This is for Mary Jane Hovanec,
the Moon Dragon.

Prologue

LIFE IS BOTH astonishingly fragile and amazingly robust at the same time. While, as far as we yet know, it can only be found on a single planet, there are few places on Earth where you can go and not find some form of life, however primitive. Even undersea volcanic vents teem with life. There are places deep within the Earth where creatures and plants live, never seeing the sun.

And yet . . . what is it that gives birth to life? What spark is it that makes a collection of chemical processes become more than simply random events? And, more than that, what is it that gives some life-forms the self-

awareness that marks them as intelligent beings?

Are these processes unique to humans? Answering that question may explain what it means to be *human.*

Computers are intelligent. Many are far more intelligent than humans. But they are not human.

But is it possible that—one day—they could *be?*

CHAPTER 1

IT AWOKE SUDDENLY. For a second it was completely confused as input flooded its senses: ocular receptors registered light and shadow; blinking, it began to channel the flood of data. Visual reconnaissance indicated a ceiling covered with acoustic tiles and suspended halogen lamps. Then, closer, life forms peering down, observing. Sentient life forms of a fairly evolved type. Homo sapien. Human. They were . . . *people.*

There were smells it classified quickly: sterilization chemicals, several forms of lubricants. A faint scent of some kind of organic-based nutrient, also. But what?

There were accoustical disturbances, from least to most intrusive: *noises*. A soft sighing: air filter. Low electronic humming: diagnostic and monitoring equipment. Its sense of touch indicated that many of these were connected to its body through stick-on sensors.

And something else: rapid inhalation and exhalation. Source? The humans. All signs indicated elevated heart rates coupled with rapid respiration. The humans appeared to be in a highly agitated or excited state.

The faces began communicating. He deconstructed the words instantly: standard English, North American sub-variety.

"—appears to be aware, Dr. Naughton."

That face he recognized as being female. The clues were obvious: lack of facial hair, eye shape, and the tone and range of the voice consistent with female vocal patterns.

"The mental processors should be on-line," the one called *Naughton* answered. He bent forward. "Yes, the eyes are following movement."

This was clearly a male. There was no facial hair, but a subcutaneous scan revealed that the hair had been scraped off. A micro-enhanced scan indicated that the sheared hair was already starting to grow back. The voice was lower in timbre, too, consistent with male vocal patterns.

"Is he awake?"

A third voice! It could only see two humans. This third voice was a cross between the male and female.

A voice recognition test indicated an adolescent male. Twelve years old. A *child*. This child was the main source of the excited breathing.

"It's not a *he*, Adam," Dr. Naughton protested.

"Well, you'll have to call it *something*," the female said with a laugh. "He needs a name."

Naughton sighed. "Even you're projecting human attributes on it," he complained. "But, very well—a name." He looked at it. "Your name is Roger."

It processed the name. *Roger*. Roger.

"Does he understand you, Dad?" asked the child.

"I sincerely hope so." Dr. Naughton checked the diagnostic monitors plugged into Roger. "Everything looks fine. Why hasn't he spoken?"

The female laughed again. Roger experienced an odd sensation. He *liked* it. "Because you haven't talked *to* him yet, Doctor," she suggested, correctly. The conversation so far had been directed around Roger, and not to him. There had been no call for a response. The female leaned forward, and Roger could smell a lingering scent of lilac on her. He liked that, too. "Can you hear us, Roger?"

"Yes," he replied.

"All right!" the child exclaimed happily. "Dad, you really did it! He's awake!"

"Well," Naughton said cautiously, "we'll have to check him out, of course, to make sure Roger is working properly, and not just saying things at random. But I'd agree, it certainly looks like we've not been wasting our time." He looked at Roger. "Do you know what you are and why you're here, Roger?"

He considered the questions for a moment. He ran them through his memory, but came up empty. "No," he said.

Dr. Naughton nodded. "Understandable, since that information hasn't been programmed into you yet. Roger, you are a machine that my assistants and I have created. Technically, you are an android. Do you know what an android is?"

Roger answered: "A robot constructed to look and act like a human being."

"Right." Dr. Naughton smiled. "And that's what you are. A machine that looks like a person, and is programmed to act like one."

"Here," said the female. She held a mirror in her hand. "Take this and look at yourself."

Roger saw a human face gazing back at him from the mirror. A child, about the same age as the Adam unit. It had mid-length fair hair, and blue eyes. Roger. He looked fully human. "This is . . . interesting," he said, handing back the mirror. "I am an Adam unit?"

"No!" Dr. Naughton looked startled. "The Adam . . . *Adam* is a human child. *You* are a replica of a human child. Do you understand the difference?"

"Of course," Roger answered. He had made a logical mistake, and filed this away for future reference. "He is real, while I am artificial."

"That's right," said Dr. Naughton, greatly relieved.

"I am your designer and creator. My name is Doctor Brewster Naughton. Adam is my son. This," he gestured at the female, "is Doctor Elizabeth Bradley. She is primarily responsible for the design of your mental processing circuitry. You have an incredibly sophisticated computer for a mind, one that will enable you to think as quickly as a human being, and react accordingly."

Roger understood. He was a machine, created by these people in their own likeness. He frowned slightly. "For what purpose did you create me?" he asked. "What is my function?"

"Interesting question," Dr. Bradley said. "Something we all want to know."

"Then let's answer it," Dr. Naughton said. "Roger, you have been created because we wanted to be sure that it was possible to create an android. You are the first we have ever assembled and fully activated. You are our prototype. And if you work out the way we sincerely hope, you will be the first of many."

"I am . . . unique?" Roger asked.

"Correct—for now." Dr. Naughton smiled. "So we're going to be studying you a lot. We have to find out if we've succeeded in making you as like a human child as we possibly can. It will mean a lot of tests, and work. You don't mind that, do you?"

"Mind?" Roger was confused. "If you created me to test me, then that is my function. I would have to be malfunctioning to object."

"I like that attitude!" Dr. Bradley said, with a grin. "And I'm going to take advantage of it, trust me."

"But I can play with him, right, Dad?" asked Adam.

"Of course you can, son," said Dr. Naughton. "That's an important part of the testing process. We have to be certain that he can pass as fully human before we can let him go with you out into the world."

Out into the world. The concept intrigued him. His memory disks were loaded with data about the world. It would be interesting to access that knowledge first-hand. He wished to have—he scanned his memory for the right word. Yes. He wished to have . . . *experiences.*

The testing *was* long and thorough. Adam was sent away for long periods of time, while Dr. Naughton and Dr. Bradley poked and prodded. Roger found some of the tests strange, but he did as he was told every time. Presumably the purpose for these tests was evident to his creators.

While he was being tested, he learned a great deal about himself. There was little in his memory concerning androids. He asked why this was. Elizabeth Bradley smiled. "Because you're the first, Roger. There isn't really any information on you yet. You'll have to add it to your memory as you go along."

"But I don't function as normal children do?" he asked.

"No," she agreed. "You mimic their functions, but your body is very different from theirs. For instance, everything needs energy to exist. Children get their energy, as you should know, from ingesting food, and breaking it down in their bodies chemically. This releases the energy they need to live."

"However," Dr. Naughton added, "this was far too complex for us to even consider replicating in your body. So instead, your energy comes from a very small battery that we've placed inside your thorax. Your replicated skin has photoreceptors in it that gather in solar energy, and they charge the battery up during the day. So you don't need to eat or drink."

"And so you don't have a sense of taste," added Dr. Bradley. "It would have been pointless to try to duplicate."

"I am inferior to real children?" Roger asked. It was a notion that intrigued him.

"In some ways, yes," Dr. Naughton admitted. "But you are superior to them in others. For example, your skeleton isn't made of bone but of high-density tungsten steel. It's far more durable than a human being's. You're not at all likely to ever break any of your bones, short of having a tank run over you. And it makes you far stronger than a human being."

"So there's good news and bad news, so to speak," Dr. Bradley added. "You lack some things people have, but have some things people lack. You're *not* a human being, don't forget, but a *simulation* of a human being. You're meant to look and act like one, not *be* one."

Roger nodded that he understood. It was going to be educational to discover these differences. He was looking forward to it.

Dr. Naughton and Dr. Bradley seemed to be pleased with his tests, and finally they allowed Adam back in to talk to Roger. Roger was pleased, because he wanted to examine the human child and see what he might discover about their similarities and differences.

Adam seemed a bit subdued when he came back, though. "Is he *safe*?" he demanded, looking at Roger oddly.

Dr. Naughton sighed. "You've been watching too much bad TV, I see," he said quietly. "Adam, Roger is absolutely safe. We've built a lot of restraints into his logic paths. He can't even think about harming you or anyone else. Remember those stories by Isaac Asimov I had you read?"

"The robot stories?"

"Right. Well, we incorporated Asimov's Three Laws into Roger here." He patted Roger's hand. "He can't harm a human, or allow one to come to harm. And he will preserve himself only when it doesn't contradict the first law."

Adam scowled. "What about the other one? Obeying all orders he's given?"

"Well," Dr. Naughton said slowly, "that's not there. You see, until he's learned a lot more about life, Roger could get into trouble if he obeyed all orders he was given. For example, what would happen if someone told him to get lost? He'd have to obey it. Since he's going to be around kids a lot, we figured that we'd give him the inclination to obey orders, but to use his best judgment before doing so."

"In other words," Elizabeth Bradley added, "if you were thinking that you'd got your own personal slave, you're out of luck. Roger will make his own mind up about things."

Roger had been reluctant to break into this conversation, but something had been said that intrigued him, and he wanted to check it out. "I am to be around children?" he asked.

"That's right," Dr. Naughton answered. "As soon as we're certain that everything is okay with you, you're going to be going to school with Adam."

"School?" Roger accessed his memories. A building where children were taught to become productive members of society. "That should be interesting."

"That's *one* word for it," said Adam. "Not the one I'd pick, though. But I guess you'll have fun coming to terms with it."

Fun was in his vocabulary, of course, but Roger had no practical idea what the word meant. Perhaps he would learn that, along with everything else, at this school he was to attend.

CHAPTER 2

ROGER HADN'T KNOWN quite what to expect from school. Well, that wasn't strictly true: from his memory banks (housed in his chest, since he had no need to breathe, and thus no lungs), he knew what school was. But he also knew, for example, what a lion was, and *knowing* couldn't possibly prepare you for *meeting* one.

Dr. Naughton and Dr. Bradley accompanied him and Adam to school on the first day. There were lots of other children there, all of them real. Roger examined them all curiously, amazed to discover that a lot of them appeared . . . odd. They had defects. A number of children had sores on their skin.

"Are these units diseased?" Roger asked.

"Zits," Adam explained. "A lot of kids get them. They're really gross to have to put up with."

"And those children with metallic mouths?" asked Roger. "They are androids, too? Earlier models, perhaps?"

"No," Adam chuckled. "They're just kids who have to wear braces. To straighten out their teeth."

"Oh." Roger frowned thoughtfully. "They are defective. This is how they are being repaired?"

"Yes."

"It seems inefficient," Roger remarked.

"Welcome to the real world," said Adam.

The other kids stared at Roger just as much. Only most of them didn't seem to be so much interested as worried. Roger couldn't understand their concern, but it became clear later. Dr. Naughton and Dr. Bradley went to homeroom with Roger and Adam. The teacher, Ms. Ellis, introduced the scientists, and then Roger. She stumbled over what to call Roger, and hastily allowed Dr. Naughton to take over.

"Roger is an android," he explained carefully. "An artificial replica of a human being. He *looks* like a human being, but he's actually all artificial. He's programmed to act and think like a person, so you won't have any trouble if you treat him like one."

A heavyset boy raised his hand. "But he's just, like, a computer on legs, right?"

"Sort of," agreed Dr. Naughton. "But he's far more sophisticated than any computer you may deal with. He can make decisions, and think logically. He's the next best thing to a human being."

"*Is* there a next best thing to a person?" the kid asked, rolling his eyes. "He's just a freaking machine, after all."

"He's more than that," Dr. Bradley said, clenching her teeth.

Roger observed her. He noticed that her mood had changed. He thought she seemed to be *annoyed.*

"He's no problem at all to the children, is he?" Ms. Ellis asked. "I mean, he's not *dangerous* or anything."

"Of course not," Dr. Naughton assured her. "He can't hurt anyone, because that isn't allowed in his programming. Everyone will be perfectly safe around him."

"He looks creepy," one girl said, shuddering. "I don't want him near me."

"That's all right, Amanda," Ms. Ellis said quickly. "He'll be seated next to Adam. You don't have to associate with him if you don't want to."

"That's the whole point of having him here," Dr. Bradley objected. "Roger is *programmed*, but we need to see how he adapts to the real world. There will be more androids made, and we want to learn all we can about improving them."

"Why improve them?" the heavyset boy sneered.

"We don't even want that one here, let alone any more."

"Because," explained Dr. Naughton, "there is a problem with babies. Some human beings can't have them any longer. For the first time ever in human history, fewer people are being born than are dying."

Another girl stuck up her hand. "My mom said that's a good thing. She says there are too many people on the Earth anyway, and we were hurting it. Now that there's less, it'll be better for the world."

"That's true in one respect," agreed Dr. Naughton. "But the problem is a continuing one. Fewer children are being born to people now, and fewer will be born when those children grow up and have children. Eventually, that means that the human race will die out."

"I don't get it," another boy complained. "What does that have to do with Freaky Fred there?"

"*Roger*," Dr. Naughton replied, "is simply a machine that will make adults feel better. Adults *need* to have children around, because it makes them feel better. There are no children left to adopt any more, and some people still want them. So we're going to build androids for those people. The androids will be like having real children around, and will make people happy again."

"But it doesn't solve the problem," the boy argued. "People will still have less kids."

"That's true," Dr. Bradley said. "There are top scientists working on solving that problem, though.

Meanwhile, Roger and others like him will help people to cope until the problem can be cured. So we need you all to treat Roger as if he were a real boy, and that way he can grow."

"Grow?" another girl asked. "But he's a *machine*. Machine's don't grow."

"Well, not physically," agreed Dr. Bradley. "He'll stay the way he looks now until he wears out or is scrapped. But his *mind* can grow. He's got a very sophisticated computer inside him that can learn and adapt. That's what can grow, and that's what we need your help with. Once we see how Roger copes, we can program the next generation of androids even better, so they'll be even more like humans."

Ms. Ellis looked worried. "He's got a computer mind?" she asked. "Won't that cause a few problems?"

"I wouldn't think so," Dr. Naughton answered, confused. "Like what?"

"Well, I can hardly give him a test with the rest of the class, can I? If he's got a computer mind, he'll *know* the answers."

Dr. Bradley grinned. "Well, he'll certainly be a straight-A student."

"But is that *fair*?" asked Ms. Ellis. "I mean, the others have to study hard and then take tests. If he's got a computer mind, he doesn't need to study."

"Actually, he does," Dr. Naughton answered. "He doesn't know *everything*. But you're right that he'll never forget something he's learned, either. I suppose it would be kind of foolish to make him take exams."

"No fair!" the heavyset kid yelled. "Why should he get special treatment just because he's an android? I'm going to complain to my folks about this! If he doesn't have to take tests, then neither should we!"

Elizabeth Bradley heaved a sigh. "He doesn't have to go to the bathroom, either," she said. "Do you want to give that up, too?" That brought a snicker from the class.

Ms. Ellis pulled a worried face. "He doesn't? Then what about eating?"

"He doesn't need to," Dr. Bradley answered. "Which means he's probably the only student here who won't complain about the food in the cafeteria." That got another laugh, but again it seemed to bother the teacher.

"Are there any other things he doesn't do?" she asked.

"Quite a few," Dr. Naughton answered. "He doesn't sweat, or cry. His nose won't run, and he'll never get sick."

"Unless he catches a computer virus!" one of the boys yelled out, which made the whole class roar.

"He only *looks* human," Dr. Naughton continued. "It's not even skin deep. His bones, for example, are metal."

"Metal?" That certainly worried Ms. Ellis. "But . . . but that's terrible."

"I don't see why," Dr. Bradley objected. "It means he can't break a leg like everyone else, but—"

"And he *certainly* can't be allowed to play games with the others," the teacher snapped. "If one of the real children ran into him, *they* could break a bone."

Roger concluded that this was true. Human children tended to mass around one hundred pounds or less. Because of his structure, he weighed over two hundred. A human child could be damaged in a collision with him.

"Sports are out," Ms. Ellis decided. She frowned. "Besides which, I would think that his computer brain would give him an unfair advantage when it came to shooting hoops and things like that. And what about swimming?"

Dr. Bradley shook her head. "His skin is waterproof, but I'm not sure that I'd want to push it too far. It's probably safer for him to stay on land."

"I should imagine!" Ms. Ellis said tartly. "If he were to short-circuit in the pool, he might well electrocute the other children."

Dr. Naughton intervened. "You're getting a trifle melodramatic," he assured her. "His batteries are low voltage, and wouldn't cause a problem. But you're right, he shouldn't play sports or go swimming."

"Great," the heavyset kid sneered. "He's gotten out of tests and gym already. This is major unfair. How come *he* gets to skip the stuff *we* have to suffer through?"

"He's just lucky, I guess," Dr. Bradley answered. "But if you give him a chance, I'm sure you'll find he's an okay person to be around. I've been with him a while now, and he's a very pleasant person."

"He's not a person," one of the girls said. "He's a *machine*."

"Try and treat him as if he *is* a person, okay?" asked Dr. Naughton.

"It's not okay," the heavyset boy answered. "He's already getting special treatment, the creep."

Based on the data collected so far, Roger computed that this was not going to be as simple an assimilation as his creators had assumed. The human children resented him. He could not understand their hostility. Didn't they understand that his not being allowed to play sports and take tests was a *punishment* for him, not a *privilege*? He wished he could join in and be as human as they were. But that was impossible.

It was time to start lessons, though, and Dr. Naughton and Dr. Bradley had to leave. "You'll do fine, I know," Dr. Bradley told him. "You can tell us all about it when you come home tonight. Have fun."

Roger scanned his memory for a definition of *fun*.

History was up first. The subject was ancient history. The teacher, Mr. Murphy, asked, "What was the name of the Persian king who fought a war against the Greeks?"

Roger answered, "Xerxes."

One kid sneered. "Show off." There was nothing

Roger didn't know. All through the lesson the teacher would ask a question and Roger would put up his hand. But Mr. Murphy wouldn't call on him. After the fifth time, Mr. Murphy sighed, and looked at Roger.

"It wouldn't be fair to ask you the answer, Roger," he said. "Because you *know* it. I have to ask one of the human children."

"But either they know it or they don't," Roger protested. "If they know it, then they are like me, and shouldn't be asked. And if they don't, isn't it foolish to ask them?"

That elicited a snicker from most of the class, but Mr. Murphy was not amused. "The whole point of asking questions is to discover what they know and understand," he answered crossly. "Not what they can get out of a computer. Stop raising your hand, and let me run the class properly."

It still felt unfair to Roger, but he understood that the teacher was in charge, and that he had to obey the teacher's instructions. Reluctantly, he had to sit by while the other children fumbled for answers to questions they did not know. Roger found the whole experience . . . *exasperating*.

After the class was over, they had to head for the science lab. Adam led the way, only to have the heavyset kid block his way. "It's the andy lover," the kid sneered. "What's up, real people not good enough for you?"

Adam went red, which was something humans could

do and Roger couldn't. He didn't have the blood vessels to produce such an effect. "Knock it off, Kenny," Adam growled.

"What's daddy going to build for you next?" Kenny mocked. "A girlfriend? A metal thing to kiss?" The other kids in the hall started to laugh.

"Don't you like *real* people?" asked Amanda.

"Just shut up," Adam snapped, his face blazing. "Come on, Roger, let's get to class. These dweebs don't matter."

Roger didn't understand why Adam was acting like this, but he decided he must have his reasons. "Of course," he agreed pleasantly, and moved forward.

Kenny moved to block his way, bumping into him in what was obviously meant to look accidental. Roger's skin sensors felt the collision, but it didn't hurt him, of course. But it hurt Kenny. The boy howled, and fell back, clutching his arm.

"He broke my arm!" Kenny howled. "He *pushed* me, and broke my arm!"

Mr. Murphy, the history teacher, came running down the hall. "What happened?" he demanded.

"That robot smacked into me and broke my arm!" Kenny screamed, clutching his shoulder.

"That is untrue," Roger said. "He collided with me deliberately. And I do not believe it was with sufficient force to damage any part of him."

The teacher looked as if he were completely out of his depth. "Kenny, go to the nurse and have your arm checked. Roger . . ." He shook his head. "We'd better go and see the principal."

"Marvelous," muttered Adam. "Your first day here, and you're already in trouble."

"But I did nothing wrong," objected Roger. "The Kenny unit caused the problem by attempting to push me aside."

"That's for the principal to decide," Mr. Murphy said. "He'll have to judge which of you is telling the truth. And his name is 'Kenny,' not 'the Kenny unit.' "

"Fact: I cannot lie," Roger said. "Kenny can. The truth is obvious, is it not? Even to your human brain?"

"Uh, can it," Adam said quietly as he stepped between them. He tried to talk reality to Roger, not logic. "The truth isn't what's at stake here. It's a human being's word against an android's. That's the problem."

"This is not fair," Roger protested.

"Welcome to the real world," Adam answered with a sigh.

CHAPTER 3

FIVE YEARS PASSED. In those five years, Adam grew and moved on. He was still Roger's best—and, for most of the time, only—friend, but unlike an android, he aged. He was now seventeen, and had been accelerated and passed the entrance exams for Harvard University. Like his father, Adam was studying cybernetics.

"I want to help create better androids," Adam explained to Roger. "Not that I mean there's anything wrong with you, of course," he added hastily.

"I am not upset," Roger replied honestly. "I know I am a primitive model. The newer ones your father is making are more sophisticated than I am. It is only to be expected that improvements will be made."

Adam smiled. "I find myself sometimes forgetting that you're not human," he confessed. "A human would be offended if anyone suggested he was less of a man than others."

"Then it is probably a good thing I'm only an android," Roger replied. "I cannot be offended."

Adam looked at him carefully. "Do you feel *any* emotions?" he asked.

"Some," Roger admitted. "Your father programmed me to be curious, so I feel that frequently. Everything interests me, and I feel . . . satisfaction when I achieve my goals, and frustration when I do not. But I cannot feel emotions like love or anger, because they have not been programmed into me. I do believe I am better off for that."

"Why do you say that?"

Roger considered his answer. "Because humans direct their emotions inappropriately. They are forever calling the android children *andys*. I understand this to be an insulting racial stereotype, along the lines of calling an Asiatic child a—"

"I get the picture!" Adam said hastily. "Yes, I've heard the term, too, and it's definitely meant to hurt."

Roger shook his head. It was a human gesture he had adopted as a means of conveying frustration and helplessness. "It is foolish, because it cannot hurt an android to be called names."

"I know, but people who use it are ignorant, and cannot see this. Besides, they use it just as much to remind themselves that they're still superior to an android because they're flesh and blood, and you're not."

Roger nodded. "I can see that this is an important distinction," he agreed. "They are produced of human parents, and carried to term in a womb. Androids are constructed in a factory. We are clearly inferior."

"It's not your fault," Adam said sympathetically. "But it doesn't have to stay that way. One of the reasons I'm studying robotics is to see if I can improve on androids by giving them simulated emotions. If you can *feel*, then you'll be closer to human."

"And is that a good thing?" asked Roger.

"Yes." Adam paced his room for a moment. "Dad's managed to do a lot of improvements over you so far. Like building an android that can lie when it's necessary."

Roger was puzzled. "That is an improvement?"

"Sometimes." Adam laughed. "Roger, do you love me?"

"I cannot," Roger answered. "I have not been programmed to love."

"There you go, you see," Adam said. "The absolute truth. It doesn't bother me, of course, because I know that. But a lot of parents buy androids as sons or daughters, and they *need* to hear that these children love them. So being able to lie means that such androids can say that they love their owners."

"And the owners accept this, even knowing that it must be a lie?"

"People believe what they want to believe," Adam said sadly. "They hear their android child say 'I love you' and they believe it, even if in their hearts they know it can't be true. They *want* to believe it. What I want to do is to make androids who can say 'I love you' to their parents and *mean* it."

Roger was thoughtful for a moment. "It seems a more honest and honorable solution," he agreed. "And far more desirable."

"My thoughts exactly." Adam gave Roger a hug. "I know you can't love me, Roger," he said. "But I do feel an odd affection for you. I guess I can understand why people want android children. And more and more than ever."

That much Roger could understand. Dr. Naughton had become very rich from his work. Fewer and fewer human children were being born with each passing year. Demand for artificial replacements had risen dramatically. Roger was now one of seven android children in a class of twenty.

And that was one of the things that bothered Roger. Dr. Naughton and Dr. Bradley had always encouraged him to speak up about anything that concerned him. Adam was on his way to Harvard University. Roger was returning to school, too.

Back to the seventh grade. Again.

"This is very inefficient," he explained to Dr. Bradley at breakfast. Naturally, he didn't need to eat, but human beings did. Dr. Bradley had been taking breakfast with them for the past two years, ever since she and Dr. Naughton had married. Roger understood that marriage was a committment between human beings, which meant that two people would promise to be faithful to one another and would live together constantly. It had seemed very sensible to Roger that Dr. Naughton and Dr. Bradley should undergo this pairing, since they were together so much anyway. But his approval of their union had caused a great deal of laughter.

"What's inefficient?" Dr. Bradley asked him, scooping out more of her grapefruit. "Eating food?"

"No, that is very sensible for humans," Roger answered. "If you did not eat, you would cease to function. And, unlike an android, you could not be repaired by replacing a power pack. No, what is inefficient is for me to retake seventh grade yet again. I do not forget the lessons I have already learned five times. My time could be better spent."

Elizabeth lay down her spoon. "I suppose that's true enough, Roger. At least, it would be if the point of your going to school was that you should learn information. But that isn't why you do it."

"I cannot see that I am doing anything else," he objected.

"Well, you are," she informed him. "You have to stay in seventh grade for legal reasons. It took enough doing to get androids to be allowed to attend school at all, you know. Schools are funded by tax payers, and a lot of them objected to tax dollars being spent to educate a bunch of robots. I suppose I can see their point, really, but the issue's a lot more complex than they try and make it appear."

Roger nodded. "And that is why Dr. Naughton subsidizes the local school system from his profits," he said. He hadn't been told this, but he was proud that he'd been able to work it out. "To keep down everyone else's taxes, so that they won't complain."

Dr. Bradley laughed. "Well, essentially that's exactly it. You're starting to understand politics. Anyway, the reason you're at school isn't so that *you* will learn. It's so that the *children* will learn from you. They have to get used to seeing androids and treating them as . . . equals."

That made a certain amount of sense, but it wasn't enough. "There are other androids now in my class," he pointed out. "It does not have to be me there. I could be doing other things, more useful things."

She bit her lower lip and then sighed. "No, that's the problem—you can't. Roger, according to the law, androids are *property*. You're simply machines made to look like people. But you *aren't* people, and you never will be. When an android is made, it is registered and locked in. You were registered as a seventh grader, and that is what you must stay. I'm sorry, but legally there's nothing else you can do. No matter how unproductive it is for you, you *have* to keep going to the same school each and every year."

Roger felt again that odd sensation that was called *disappointment.* His gloomy mood stayed with him all the way to school.

"Good morning, Roger."

"Good morning, Brittany," he replied. She was another android, and this was the third year they had been together. "Though I am not sure just how good it is."

She frowned slightly. "Is there a problem?"

"This is the fifth time I am taking the seventh grade," he complained. "It all seems so futile."

Brittany nodded. "Yes, I agree. But it is what we must do."

"But *why* must we do it?" he asked. "Just because we are property, and our owners insist on it?"

"Yes," she said simply.

"It is inefficient and foolish," he argued.

At that moment, a group of real kids sauntered over. These had to be the new students for this semester, because Roger didn't recognize any of them. But he recognized the type: these were all like Kenny. They had hostile expressions on their faces. Roger had seen that look many times before.

"Stinking andys," the leader of them sneered. "They should never allow them into schools with *real* kids."

Roger stared at the boy. Normally, he would simply ignore such a comment. He'd heard it often enough in five years. But today he felt frustrated, and he decided that it was time to reply. "You are afraid because you are inferior to us," he answered. "You resent us because we are better than you."

The boy's expression went from hostile through shock to fury. "Filthy little monster!" he screamed. "I'll show you!" With a snarl, he jumped forward, swinging his fist.

Roger moved swiftly, blocking the blow with his hand. "If you hit me, you will break your hand," he said calmly. "This is not a wise move."

As it was, the boy howled with pain. The other children in the circle shouted and jeered. One of them snatched up a fallen branch and rushed at Roger, whirling the stick around. Roger was taken by surprise by the boy's actions, and hesitated. The boy slammed down with all of his strength as Roger blocked the blow with his left arm.

The stick cracked and shattered, but not before it did some damage. Roger couldn't feel pain, of course, but he could sense the breakage. One of the links to his wrist was crushed by the blow, and his arm locked into place. Seeing him damaged, the rest of the boys jumped into the fight, hitting him with books or anything else they had in their bags. Roger was hampered in two ways: first, by the injury to his arm, and second, by his programming. He was not allowed to injure a human being.

The human children, however, had no such programming concerning androids.

Roger was stronger and heavier than the boys, but he could not fight back. He staggered, impassive, but the weight of five boys brought him crashing to the ground. Yelling and shouting, the boys pummeled him with fists and sticks.

"Stop it!" Brittany ordered. When this produced no effect, she simply bent down and hauled the closest boy up and away, dropping him to the ground and then returning for the next.

"Get her!" the first boy yelled, and more kids came running to join in the one-sided fight. Several of them started to punch Brittany, who now had to protect herself as best she could. Roger was struggling to rise, but it wasn't easy without damaging a human.

"Enough!" an adult voice thundered. "Stop this at once, all of you!"

It was the assistant principal, a large man named Wilkins. He glared down at everyone. The children didn't dare disobey him, and they reluctantly stopped what they were doing and clambered to their feet.

"He started it," the first kid snarled.

"He's an android," Mr. Wilkins answered coldly. "He couldn't possibly have started a fight. And I know you well, Michael. You're a born troublemaker."

"You're on the stinking andys' side!" Michael complained. "Andy lover."

"You'd better stop talking right now," he said. "Before you say something that I'll be forced to discipline you for additionally." He glowered at the seven boys. "All of you, report to the principal's office." He looked at Roger. Brittany had helped him to his feet, but his arm was still locked into place. "You'd better report to the nurse's office, I suppose."

"You mean the scrap heap," muttered Michael. Mr. Wilkins gave him a cold stare.

Brittany helped Roger to the nurse's office. This wasn't quite as silly as it might have sounded, because there were now almost a hundred androids in the school. Though they were all very strong and quite tough, there were sometimes accidents that required repair. Besides the nurse, the school employed an android technician—a repairman. He whistled when Roger came in.

"You've been in the wars, looks like," he said. "I'm Gilbert Chin. On the bed. Hmmm . . ." He did a quick examination. "Broken servo, shorted linkage. And some epidermal damage. If I didn't know better, I'd say you've been in a fight."

"I have," Roger confessed. "Though I was not the one fighting."

"Ah." The technician started working on the arm. "Trouble with the kids?"

"There is always trouble with human children," Brittany complained. "They resent us, and try to provoke us constantly. They want to damage us."

"Not all of them," Chin answered, taking out the

broken linkage. "Most kids are pretty cool."

"Their body temperatures are an irrelevant consideration in the present discussion," said Brittany.

The man had to stifle a laugh.

"There are human children who are deliberately nasty," Roger said.

"There always have been," he said. "Look, I'm from Chinese parents. When they were kids, the other children in their school called them names, and tried to pick fights with them, just because they looked different. The same thing happened to Black kids, and Latino kids. Children do this. They pick a minority group and focus their anger on those people. It's something a lot of kids go through. Hopefully, they'll grow out of it."

"But why do they do it?" asked Roger, puzzled.

"Because they're afraid," the technician said. "Because they want to feel better about themselves. They make somebody else a target, calling them inferior, because it gives them someone to feel superior to."

Roger felt another new emotion then: *guilt.* "Then the fight was my fault," he said slowly. "When they insulted me, I told them that they were jealous of me because I am better than they are. I, too, am guilty of their crime."

"Not a smart thing to say," the man agreed, testing the new linkage. "But in your case, you were only stating the truth. They couldn't take it." He lowered his voice. "Take my advice, though, and watch what sort of truths you tell, okay?"

"I shall," Roger promised. He had a lot to think about.

After the repairs were finished, he and Brittany went back to class. Michael and the other boys were there, and they were clearly not happy. Roger apologized for being late, and Ms. Ellis told them to sit down.

"The andy's got a girlfriend," Michael sneered.

"Maybe they've been kissing," giggled one of his friends.

"Nah," Michael said. "If they tried, they'd give each other a shock."

"That's quite enough talking," Ms. Ellis snapped. "I'll bear you both in mind when it comes to questions, though. Right, everyone, pay attention. . . ."

Roger didn't have to, of course. He'd been through all of the classes enough times already. Instead, he sat, thinking about what had happened. Were human children really so prejudiced against androids? And, if so, could anything ever be done to change their attitudes?

He felt glum. Maybe things would never change. Maybe this was all there was.

For the second time that morning Roger experienced a new sensation. And this sensation had a name, too. It was called . . . *forever*.

CHAPTER 4

ANOTHER FIVE YEARS passed by. In some ways, Roger reflected, they went swiftly. But in others, they dragged and dragged. He'd taken ten years of seventh grade now, and was doomed to continue the same routine over and over again.

"I think this is what the humans mean by Hell," Brittany had told him at one point. He found himself inclined to agree.

But some things did change. Dr. Naughton was going gray, and getting more and more frustrated. Roger found it better to avoid talking to him [illegible] possible because he was [illegible]

to Dr. Bradley. She had changed, too, in the ten years since Roger's awakening. She had put on a little weight, and her once-long hair was now trimmed short. She tired more easily, too, but she always had time for him. He found himself wondering if this was how human mothers were with their children.

There were good changes, too. Adam had finished his university education, and had graduated with honors. Roger was not surprised, since he knew how clever Adam was, but he was pleased. Even better, it meant that Adam was coming home again, since he was going to work with his father now. He'd see more of his first human friend. Adam, of course, had changed greatly. He was now twenty-two, and very different from the boy Roger had first known.

But Roger, of course, was unchanged. He was still a twelve-year-old. At least on the outside.

When Adam returned home, he was happier than Roger could ever recall him being before. Part of that was due to the fact that he could now start working instead of studying, but another part was clearly because of Anthea.

"I met her at Harvard," Adam explained over dinner. Roger wasn't eating, of course, but he always took his seat at the table and waited, joining in the conversation where appropriate. "We're going to be married."

"That's wonderful!" Dr. Bradley exclaimed happily. [illegible]r in offering his congratulations, Roger noticed. He found his reticence puzzling.

Anthea was studying to become a molecular biologist. She and Adam had taken some classes together. Anthea smiled. "We were attracted to one another immediately and, well, one thing led to another. And here we are." Roger was pleased for Adam. He clearly had a great deal of affection for Anthea. She was bright, personable and, he supposed, very pretty.

He simply couldn't understand this human need for attachment to another person. After dinner, he questioned Adam about it. Adam was in a very good mood, and was amused by Roger's curiosity.

"Marriage has two different purposes," he explained. "First, when people fall in love, they want to be together as much as possible. Marriage is their way of telling the world that they do love one another and want to stay together."

"Like your father and Dr. Bradley," Roger said.

"Exactly." Adam grinned. "I never thought Dad would be the old romantic, but I'm glad I was wrong. Anyway, the other reason is to have children. Children are an expression of love, and are raised by their parents in a loving environment."

"But you were raised only by your father," Roger objected.

"Because my mother died when I was young," Adam explained. "Otherwise, she would have stayed."

Roger frowned, thinking. "Many human beings have

problems having children nowadays," he said slowly. "Does this mean that they are not then truly married?"

"No," Adam answered. "Because most of them would have children if they could. But they can't."

Anthea joined in here. She was sitting on the arm of Adam's chair. Her arm was draped over his shoulder. "That's why I'm in molecular biology," she explained. "Human beings have babies when the DNA of a mother and father join together. But if the DNA is damaged, no children can be born. And in many, many people these days, the DNA is very damaged indeed."

"Why is that?" Roger asked.

Anthea sighed. "A number of reasons, really. One is because human beings have polluted the world so much with industrial and chemical wastes. These get into our food and bodies, and damage human DNA. What I want to do is to try and work on methods of repairing this cellular damage, so that more people will be able to have children again."

"That sounds like an excellent idea," Roger said approvingly. "There are less and less real children in my class each year, and more and more androids. This is not a good thing."

"No," Adam agreed. "No, it isn't. Roger, you know I like you, but I'd be just as happy if we really never had to build another android."

"I understand perfectly," Roger assured him. "I do

hope that it would become unnecessary."

Anthea gave him an odd look, and then laughed. "Adam, I'm quite amazed. You told me that Roger is a primitive android, but he seems very sophisticated to me."

"Well, he's an excellent learner," Adam answered. "And Dad and Dr. Bradley are always updating him and making modifications. But his emotional circuits are crude, and his response menu is limited. But he's a good model. And once I can fit him with some of my new concept circuits, I'm sure he'll be even better."

"Will they alter me?" Roger asked curiously.

"In some ways," Adam replied. "They'll help you to simulate more emotions, and make you appear to be even more human. I'm hoping that one day nobody will be able to tell a real person from an android just by looking at or talking to them. It's not possible right now, but it might become so one day."

"I shall look forward to it."

Home life became a lot more interesting from that point on. The wedding was held inside a church. It was very elaborate, with everyone dressed in formal attire. A great deal of attention was lavished on food and beverages. There was one that Roger found especially intriguing. It was called champagne. Roger didn't drink it, of course. But it had a most remarkable effect on the humans. It made them . . . *giddy*.

Roger found the church interesting, too. It was an old building, and was filled with many beautiful ornaments and strange objects. The family didn't attend church, but Roger had knowledge of them. But that had not prepared him for experiencing one. There was no reason for Roger to attend church, of course. Only human beings believed in a God. That he found puzzling. *They* believed that they, too, were manufactured beings. They believed that a God had created them. He *knew* that a human being had created him. Was Dr. Naughton God?

The wedding was enjoyable, and then Adam and Anthea stayed together in the house with Dr. Naughton and Dr. Bradley and himself. They seemed to be very happy, and very busy. Adam worked with his father, while Anthea drove to a medical laboratory every day to work. Most days, she dropped Roger at school. He came to enjoy the rides, because he had a chance to talk to Anthea. He liked her, and she had a delight in life that he found fascinating.

School became interesting again for him. He had several friends—all androids, of course. Some human children were polite to the andys, but most simply left them alone. There were fewer and fewer really obnoxious ones, like the Kennys and Michaels. Possibly because they were outnumbered by the androids. Slightly more than half the class were androids this year. Ms. Ellis was still their teacher, though she was almost entirely white-haired now, and evidently old by human standards. Mr. Wilkins was still the principal, and Roger liked the man. He was very fair.

His best friends were Brittany and William. The three of them sat out gym together every time. Roger always hated that, because it looked like the humans were having so much fun at their games. William was especially annoyed by it.

"It makes no sense that over half the class cannot compete in sports," he pointed out. "Why not simply form android-only teams?"

"Because that's segregation," Brittany argued. "We would only be allowed to play other android teams."

"But at least we could *play*," William objected. "Instead of being forced to watch humans do something that we could do a lot better."

"Could we?" asked Roger. "I wonder. Oh, I agree that we could probably hit the balls better, and farther, if we were playing baseball. But could we make the decisions as to whether we should run as well? Humans have an edge on us in thinking."

"Not all of them," William answered. "Some of them are positively stupid, even judged by human standards." Roger knew who he meant, because there were three real kids in their class who had trouble even paying attention to the lessons. They weren't very bright, and it hardly seemed worth the trouble trying to educate them. The problem was, of course, what else was there to do with them?

Brittany looked at William with interest. "I do believe you're prejudiced against humans," she decided.

"Of course I am," William complained. "We are far

superior to them, and yet we're looked upon as nothing more than property, while the little human monsters get all of the advantages." He sighed. "My family has a son who is going to go to college next year. I've watched him grow up for eight years, and get to do things I will never be allowed to do. And he's not grateful at all. He doesn't want to study, and sees college as a time to party and date girls. What a waste!"

"Perhaps it is," agreed Roger. After all, he himself wished to advance; he couldn't fault William for wanting the same. "But this is a human world; we are here only for their convenience."

"But is that fair?" demanded William.

"It is if humans say it is," Brittany answered. "After all, we wouldn't even be here if they hadn't created us. We should be grateful for whatever we are given."

William glared at her. "Suck-up," he muttered. "I'll just bet your family loves you, if you talk like that to them."

Brittany looked puzzled. "Doesn't your family love you?"

"No. They don't like the way I speak, for one thing."

"Well, if you speak to them the way that you speak to us, you can hardly blame them," Roger informed him. "Humans want respect and gratitude."

"Shouldn't they *earn* them?" William demanded. "Anyway, my family is talking about getting rid of me."

That amazed Roger. He had never heard of such a thing. "Getting rid of you?" he repeated. "But . . . how? Why?"

"They had a dog once," William said. "I liked the silly animal, but it kept chewing the furniture. They gave it away to another family. Perhaps they see me as something like that dog, and wish to give me to another family."

"They can't mean it," protested Brittany. "You're not a dog."

"No," William agreed bitterly. "There are laws preventing cruelty to dogs. There are no laws preventing cruelty to androids."

"But surely no one would do that?" Brittany asked, astonished.

William laughed, but it was a harsh sound. "Don't you believe it," he told her. "With humans, *anything* is possible."

Roger was sure that William was exaggerating the problem. Perhaps he had been bought by a bad family, not at all like the Naughtons. What he was describing couldn't possibly happen.

But it did.

Two days later, William didn't appear at school. At first, Roger simply thought that he might be experiencing malfunctions. He always took foolish risks and sometimes damaged himself. But when he got to homeroom, he saw that William's desk was missing. He asked Ms. Ellis about it.

"William won't be coming to school again," she said. "His family decided that they no longer needed a child, with their other boy going to college. William has been reprocessed."

"Reprocessed?" Roger had never heard the term before.

"Yes," Ms. Ellis said, hesitantly. "You should ask your father about it. I'm sure he knows far more about it than I do. Now, it's time to start our lessons."

That evening, when Anthea picked him up after school, Roger asked her about reprocessing. She became distracted, and it took her a minute to focus on his question. "Where did you hear about that?" she asked.

"One of my friends at school is missing," Roger answered. "I was told that his family no longer needed him and he was reprocessed."

Anthea drove in silence for a while, and Roger could sense that she was disturbed. Finally she said: "You know that your—consciousness, shall we call it—is just a collection of programming and memories, don't you?"

"Of course," Roger answered. "Like the human consciousness."

"Well, human consciousness is a bit more complicated than that," explained Anthea. "But reprocessing takes place when a family doesn't want a particular android any longer. The android's memories are wiped, and he or she is returned to the salesroom, until they are bought by another family."

"Memories wiped?" repeated Roger. He had never considered such a thing before. "William had all of his memories removed?"

"Yes, so the next family who buys him can start all over again, without the clutter of memories from another family getting in the way."

"Memories removed . . ." Roger was appalled. "But, since we are the sum of our programming and memories, without his memories, William no longer exists. He has been destroyed."

"No, he's simply been blanked and will start again." Anthea looked at him. "Roger, it's not as big a deal as you're making it. It won't bother him, and it shouldn't worry you."

Roger was not consoled. To have one's memories wiped, to become . . . *nothing*. It was like killing a human. And it didn't seem to bother Anthea at all!

"Is that what will happen to me?" he asked. "Will I have my memories wiped when I am no longer wanted? Will I cease to exist?"

"No!" Anthea exclaimed. "Roger, nobody in the family would *ever* want to get rid of you! We love you as you are!"

"*Now* you do," Roger answered. "But will that always be the case? Anthea, I shall outlive everyone of you humans. One day, the family will be different. And they may not want me. What shall I do then?"

"Don't be silly, Roger," Anthea replied. "That could never happen to you. Don't worry about it at all."

But Roger couldn't help worrying about it. It was gnawing at him desperately, like a short-circuit that couldn't be isolated and repaired. The idea of being blanked scared him. And he'd never been afraid before.

The new processors that Adam had given him were simulating emotions really well. He had now learned *fear*.

Two months later the situation had grown worse. He greeted Brittany as they entered class together. She gave him an odd, unfriendly look.

"I don't know you," she said. "My name is Tori, not Brittany."

Roger didn't understand. Of course she was Brittany! Why was she claiming to be somebody else?

Ms. Ellis intervened. "Her name *is* Tori."

"I do not understand," he said. "My memory clearly shows that she is Brittany, my friend."

"She *was* Brittany," Ms. Ellis answered. "Until yesterday. Her parents decided that they wanted their daughter to grow up. They bought a new model android, one that is twenty-two years old, and transfered all of Brittany's memories to her. Another family bought the Brittany model, which was reprocessed. This child is now Tori."

CHAPTER 5

ROGER DIDN'T EVEN try to talk to Anthea about this when she picked him up. He was too terrified, and he wanted answers and reassurance from the top—Dr. Naughton, Dr. Bradley, and Adam. All day, his mind had been filled with terrible thoughts and fears. He was in danger of being reprocessed!

Both of his best friends were gone. Roger was next.

"Tori" had tried making friends with him, but Roger had fended off her overtures without even trying to be polite. Tori was hurt, but Roger couldn't help that. He simply couldn't bring himself to forget that just yesterday she had been Brittany—and now she wasn't.

Anthea took no notice of his emotional state. She was lost in her own thoughts. When they arrived home, they had to wait for almost two hours before Dr. Naughton, Adam and Dr. Bradley came back from their laboratory.

"I must speak with you all," Roger said, politely but firmly. "I am extremely disturbed."

Dr. Bradley looked puzzled and concerned. "By what, Roger?"

"Two of my friends have been reprocessed," he said bluntly. "One of them was bought by another family and turned up at my school today as a different person."

"And that was unsettling for you?" asked Adam.

Roger stared at him. "As unsettling as it would be for you to find that Anthea had changed personalities overnight and was now called Glenda."

Adam chuckled at the thought. "Roger, it's not like that with androids. Your personalities are just what's programmed into you. Nothing more."

"No," Roger said. "It is also what our memories have added to our programming. I am not the same android as I was when you first switched me on. I have learned and evolved."

"That's true," Dr. Bradley agreed. "But what is true for androids and what is true for humans are two very different things."

"How different?" Roger demanded. "I have feelings, too." He glared reproachfully at Adam. "You should know. You programmed most of them into me. And now I have learned fear."

Adam shook his head. "Roger, you don't have *feelings*. You have simulations of feelings. You're not human, and not alive. You are simply programmed to *act* alive."

"Perhaps there is a distinction because of that in your mind," Roger told him. "But there is not one in mine. I *feel* alive. I *feel* my emotions. Apparently, in just the way that you do. To me, they are very real. And right now I feel betrayed."

"Betrayed?" Dr. Naugthon glanced at him sharply. "That's rather a strong word."

"It's rather a strong emotion," Roger explained. "William was sold, and purged. He no longer exists. Brittany had her memory transfered to a fresh android, and her old body is now host to a new personality."

"I can see that this might be upsetting you, Roger," Dr. Bradley said. "But you'll get used to it. Brittany isn't *dead*—she's just changed. And change happens even to human beings."

"And now it happens to some androids," Roger said bitterly. "Without their consent or even knowledge."

Adam looked as though he was starting to get angry. "Only living beings need give their consent, Roger. You are just property; you have no rights."

"I am beginning to understand." He had thought

that these people were his family. How could they treat him like this? How could they care so little? "William said that he was being destroyed because he spoke up that androids had no rights. Perhaps he was correct in his belief."

Dr. Bradley looked concerned. "Roger, you don't understand."

"No," he agreed. "I don't. I had thought that androids were a loved part of the family, not simply some machine to be disposed of when their owners got tired of them, or wanted a newer model."

"And you're afraid that will happen to you?" asked Adam. He shook his head. "I give you my word, Roger: We will never purge or reprogram you. Are you happy now?"

"No!" Roger stared at him. "My friends are—" he groped for the appropriate word. "They are *dead*. How can I be happy?"

"They're not dead," Dr. Naughton said sternly, "because they were never alive to begin with. You're not *alive*. You just *think* you are."

"And what is the difference?" Roger demanded. "If I believe I am alive, wouldn't it be murder to me if you purged me?"

"We won't," Adam promised.

Roger was about to reply, when Anthea gave a sudden strangled cry, and collapsed to the floor. Instantly, all attention was on her. Adam jumped to her side, picking her up gently.

"Call the ambulance!" he cried. "We have to get her to the hospital immediately." His father jumped to the communications net panel to do this.

"What is wrong?" asked Roger. "Is she malfunctioning?"

"Not exactly," Dr. Bradley answered, taking Anthea's pulse. "She's pregnant."

"Pregnant?" Roger stared at Anthea, confused. He knew what that meant, of course: that she was going to make a baby. But he hadn't realized that she was in this state. He knew from his biology program now what was happening. She must have been feeling sick for the past couple of months. And he had been so preoccupied with his own cares that he hadn't even noticed that she had been putting on weight. "She is having the child now?"

"No." Dr. Bradley shook her head, though she was concentrating mostly on Anthea. "It's not time yet. There must be a problem."

Roger was confused. "I have more questions. Is our conversation terminated?"

Adam glared at him. "Not now, Roger. Just be quiet."

Roger was hurt, but obediently he kept silent. Looking after Anthea was the most important thing right now, he knew. His own problems could wait until she was well again.

The ambulance arrived a short while later. Adam went with Anthea to the hospital. Dr. Naughton and

Dr. Bradley followed them in their car. Roger was left at home. Roger couldn't help feeling worried about Anthea. He had liked her from the start, and she had easily accepted him as a member of the family.

But now he wondered—what sort of member of the family?

Humans were strange creatures, he knew. They spoke very easily of *love*, but they meant so many different things by it. They loved their families, of course. But they loved their pets, too—whatever families actually had pets nowadays. The same problems humans were facing with a dropping birth rate affected animals also. They also loved their cars, or their houses. They loved a good book or a TV show. They even loved old sweaters.

So . . . where did all of this leave him? He was sure that the family loved him in some way. But *what* way?

Then he felt guilty for dwelling on his own problems when Anthea was obviously damaged in some way. The family was understandably more worried about her than about him. And so should he be too.

An hour later, there was a call on the communications net. Since there was nobody at home, Roger answered it. He was hoping that it was a message from Adam or Dr. Bradley telling him that Anthea was fine.

"Roger!" she exclaimed. It was a female that he had never seen before. "I am so glad that you answered the call. I wanted to speak to you. I am Brittany."

"Brittany!" Roger stared at her face, astonished.

There was a certain resemblance to the old Brittany: the same hair color and style, and the same color eyes. But this one was older. Of course she was! She was in a twenty-something body now. "Are you fine?"

"Yes," she assured him. "You knew that I have been resettled?"

"Ms. Ellis informed me this morning," Roger answered. "There is a new girl in class with your old body. It was very unsettling."

"I imagine it must have been," Brittany agreed. She appeared to be very uncomfortable. "I am sorry you had to experience that."

"I am sorry you have had to experience reprogramming," he answered. "Was it hard for you?"

"No," she answered. "They simply disconnected my power supply, downloaded my memories into the new body and then awakened me in it. I felt no discontinuity, and am as I was before."

"I am very pleased to hear that," Roger told her honestly. "Then we can still be friends."

Brittany shook her head. "No. That is why I am calling you, Roger. I have been given a new function now. I am no longer to be in seventh grade. I am a student of the university."

"University?" Roger was confused. "But androids are not allowed to go there."

"I am to be one of the first," Brittany told him. "There are too few humans now alive to fill all the jobs that must be done. Some androids are to be trained to fill those functions. I am to learn to become a teacher, and must go away to study. My parents are very proud of me."

"I am pleased for you," Roger said. "But sad for myself. You are my friend, Brittany, and I do not wish to be parted from you."

"It is the way that things must be," Brittany answered. "We can do nothing about this."

"No," he agreed, bitterly. "We cannot. We are at the mercy of whatever the humans wish to do with us."

"It is not that bad," she assured him.

"Perhaps not for you," he countered. "But I am still in seventh grade. And I have to sit near your old body and know that I no longer have a friend. There is no way that I can convince myself that this is a good thing."

"Perhaps not," Brittany agreed sadly. "But it is a necessary thing. I shall miss you, Roger."

"I miss you already, Brittany," he replied. "Be well." He cut the connection. It was bad enough that she had been forced to change her body at a human whim, he mused angrily. Now she was being forcibly separated from her friends, so that she could serve human beings as a teacher. It was all too much to accept!

But . . . what alternative did they have? Androids could refuse to obey orders, of course. They had that much freedom. But if they refused to obey their personalities could be erased. Just like that. There was no protection for androids at all.

They were, Roger realized, slaves. Androids had no rights. A human owner could do anything it wished to an android—even destroy one—and suffer no penalty for it.

It was horrible.

Roger sat brooding for several hours. Then Dr. Naughton returned home. "How is Anthea?" he asked. Roger felt guilty that he hadn't been worrying more about Anthea.

"Hmm?" Dr. Naughton brought his attention into focus. "Oh, she's resting. Apparently she's having a problem pregnancy, but she should be fine."

"You might have called from the hospital," said Roger. "I was very worried about her health."

Dr. Naughton glared at him. "I had other concerns," he replied stiffly. "Reassuring a pan wasn't uppermost in my mind."

Roger hadn't heard that term before. "A *pan*?" he repeated, confused.

Dr. Naughton looked guilty. "I'm sorry, I shouldn't have said that. Excuse me." He brushed past Roger and into the kitchen. Roger didn't understand why he wouldn't explain himself. The doctor fixed himself a sandwich, and locked himself in his study, giving Roger firm orders not to disturb him.

Roger didn't need sleep, of course. Some evenings, he was placed on standby to conserve power, but most evenings he was simply left to his own devices. He liked to read books. The family had a large library, and Roger was making his way through it quite well, since he never forgot what his eyes scanned into his memory banks. Tonight he read books about babies. He would have to get ready for when Anthea brought hers home.

It was confusing, because it seemed as though no two authors agreed on how a baby should be looked after. Roger realized that, even after all these millions of years, human beings still didn't really understand how to raise children. Most peculiar! Well, it was obviously a lot different from raising an android! He strove to make as much sense from the books as possible, but was afraid that he was getting more and not less confused. He would have to ask Dr. Bradley's advice, he realized. And Anthea's, when she came home. Women, it appeared, understood babies better than men, even if men wrote most of the books about them.

Dr. Bradley came home halfway through the night, looking very tired. Roger changed his mind about asking her to explain about rearing babies to him. Instead, he asked her, "Would you like me to get you food or a drink? You look tired."

She seemed surprised by the offer. "That's very thoughtful of you, Roger. Yes, I'd love a pastrami on rye, and a cup of warm milk. Do you know how to make them?"

"Of course," he answered. "I have read most of the books on home care and cookery in the kitchen. I know all about food."

"Maybe we should make you the chef, then," she said. Roger thoughtfully considered her proposal.

"I should probably enjoy that," he replied. "I would like to put my learning to practical use. Of course, it is of no use to me, since I do not eat and have no taste buds. Perhaps I would not be able to correctly judge whether food I prepare is good to eat."

It was only then that Roger saw the bewildered look on her face and realized she had been joking.

"Well, I'm sure you'll have no problems fixing me a sandwich." Dr. Bradley smiled. "Thanks, Roger."

He went into the kitchen and prepared the food for her. He warmed the milk in the microwave, assembled the sandwich, and brought them both through to the living room. Dr. Bradley had kicked off her shoes and was settled back in a chair, looking extremely tired.

"Are these acceptable?" he asked her.

She took a bite of the sandwich and a sip of the milk. "Very," she assured him. "Maybe you would make a good chef, after all."

Roger nodded solemnly. "Is Anthea alright?" he asked.

She put down the glass of milk. "Well, the doctors think she'll be fine, but they really don't know yet. They've got a whole battery of tests to perform on her in the morning." She hesitated, and then went on. "She's . . . had trouble becoming pregnant. A lot of women these days have. I couldn't manage it at all. Anthea's been taking drugs to help her out."

Roger knew from his studies that drugs were designed to overcome problems in the human body. Many were benign, but some had serious side-effects. "And this has caused problems?"

"We don't know yet." Dr. Bradley ran her hand through her hair. "It's possible. The tests will tell us more in the morning. There's nothing we can do until then, except pray."

"I cannot pray," Roger said sadly. "I was made by a human being, not a God."

"That's okay," she assured him. "I'll do enough praying for the both of us. Now, if you don't mind, I'd like to be left alone."

He nodded. "I understand. But, if you will, one more, simple question: what is a *pan*?"

"A pan?" She looked at him sharply. "So you've heard somebody call you that? Well, don't let it bother you. It's just a term of ignorance. It's from the old story *Peter Pan*. That's about a boy who never grows up. Since androids can't grow up, some ignorant people call androids pans now. It's very foolish. Don't let it bother you."

"I understand," he lied. It was no real problem for him to keep his face impassive until he had left the room. Then he faltered.

A term of ignorance and prejudice? Then why had his own creator used it against him? Roger felt his whole world collapsing about him. He felt terribly betrayed.

CHAPTER 6

ROGER WAS CAUGHT in a swirl of conflicting emotions. His most recent upgrade had significantly expanded his emotional response menu. But it was still too limited and primitive to process what he was experiencing. But one thing he was sure of—the family was going through enough trouble right now without having to worry about his problems, too. He decided to keep them to himself.

Anthea was allowed to come home the next day, but she was confined to bed. And she had a private nurse to stay with her. Roger was allowed to visit and talk, but Anthea seemed very preoccupied, which was understandable. She chatted with Roger, but neither of them mentioned his problems. Nor did Anthea talk about the progress of the baby.

Dr. Naughton, Dr. Bradley, and Adam were very tense. They were all listening for the slightest sound from Anthea. Roger didn't need to be a detective to know that something serious must be wrong with the mother-to-be, but nobody ever mentioned it—at least, not while he was around. The strain in the house was growing.

He took the bus to school. It was not as enjoyable as riding in the car with Anthea. He had always looked forward to their talks. But with Anthea confined to bed, no one else had offered to drive him to school. It was just as well. Roger actually enjoyed the feeling of independence it gave him boarding the bus on his own. But his spirit darkened the minute he got on the bus. Tori was also on the bus. His first thought was to sit as far away from her as possible. But she reached up and grabbed his arm.

"Sit down!" she ordered him. Meekly, Roger obeyed. He wasn't sure why she even wanted to speak to him, considering how rude he had been to her. She studied his face and then shook her head. "It's not my fault."

"What isn't?"

"Whatever happened to your friend Brittany," she

said. "I can't help the fact that I've been given her body. I didn't ask for it."

Roger felt another new emotion—embarrassment. It seemed that he was getting an overdose of emotions these past few days! "You're right," he agreed, ashamed of his behavior. "It isn't your fault. And . . . I talked to Brittany last night. At least, I talked to what she's become. She's going away, and we can't be friends any longer."

Tori nodded slowly. "Then is there any reason why we can't be friends?"

Roger managed a wan smile. "I don't know why you'd want to be friends with me. I've been horribly rude to you."

"I guess I'm just a very forgiving person," she said. Then she hesitated. "Besides which, I don't think the reprocessing purged everything from my systems. When I first saw you, I found myself liking you. Can you possibly forget that I was once Brittany, and accept me as Tori?"

It was a good question: could he? "I cannot forget Brittany," he said honestly. "But I can accept that you are someone else, your own person. And, yes, I'd like very much to be your friend."

"Fine." She stuck out her hand. "Shake on it." Roger obeyed. Tori certainly was a different person than Brittany—and he decided he liked her.

Tori turned out to be the only good thing in his life for the next couple of months. School was, as always, monotonous. For Tori, of course, it was fresh, and Roger found new interest in showing her books and information that supplemented their lessons. He enjoyed talking to her, because she had a very fascinating personality. It didn't take him as long as he'd expected to forget the person she had once been. Tori was interested in everything, and expressed joy in it all.

Home, however, was like walking on an electrified floor. Roger never knew when and where the next shock would come from. Dr. Bradley, who had always been his favorite member of the family, became brooding and withdrawn. She started to snap at him if he even asked questions, so Roger stopped talking to her. She didn't seem to care. Dr. Naughton had never been easy to deal with, and he seemed worse than ever now. He was working longer hours, experimenting on different kinds of creations. He had given up almost entirely on making androids, leaving that to Adam and his staff. Instead, he was attempting to make a robot dog.

That alerted Roger to a fresh problem, and he did a little online research. He discovered that almost the entire dog population of the world was gone. That confused him at first, because there were still plenty of humans left, even if they were having problems having children. Then he realized, of course, that dogs had shorter lives. A human generation was about twenty-five years; a dog generation was about three.

He talked about this with Tori, and she confirmed

his suspicions. "My parents are veterinarians," she explained. "They used to have a very busy business. Now they get two or three patients a week."

"It's not just dogs, then?" he asked, appalled.

"Roger, it's *every* living thing." It was hard to believe that she was, objectively, just a few weeks old, and he was over twelve. Sometimes she seemed to be so much more mature than him. It was simply a matter of her more sophisticated circuitry, of course, but Roger felt rather embarrassed. She smiled sadly at him and patted his hand. "Human beings spent many thousands of years polluting the world," she explained. "They didn't have a terrible problem until there were enough of them to make a huge impact, so most of it has been in the last hundred years or so. They've put so many poisons into the natural world that it's caused a lot of problems. Mercury and many of the rare earth metals are poisonous to living creatures. Fish and small birds and insects ingest the poisons and die. They're eaten by predators, which get poisoned in their turn."

"I know that," Roger said. "But the dumping of poisons has stopped. There should be less and less each year. Things should be able to start living longer again."

"You'd think so, wouldn't you?" she asked. "But it doesn't work like that. The poisons also affect the DNA—the basic building blocks of life that animals use to reproduce. The DNA is changed, and animals can't reproduce properly. As a result, fewer and fewer young are born, and many of the ones that are born are malformed or sick. Fifty years ago, kids were finding frogs with five legs in some ponds because they'd been poisoned before birth. Nowadays, almost everything has that kind of problem."

Every living thing on Earth? thought Roger. Slowly dying out . . . "Can't anything be done about it?" he asked.

"People are trying," Tori informed him. "But they're working on *people*. Not animals. They're not considered a high priority." She touched his hand again. "Come home with me tonight. I want to show you something."

Roger was surprised by her offer. Nobody had ever asked him to come home with them before. Human children did that kind of thing all of the time, but androids didn't tend to socialize with one another—and few human kids wanted to associate with androids.

At that moment, a small group of real kids came past where Roger and Tori were sitting. "Look at that," one of them sneered. "Two pans, trying to act human."

"Idiots," muttered Tori. "Ignore them, Roger. They don't know any better."

Roger was amazed again, to hear her so critical of humans. "You shouldn't say things like that," he whispered back, watching the children retreat, laughing. "You'll get into trouble."

"Maybe," she agreed. "But they *are* idiots."

Then Tori did something extraordinary. She giggled.

The front rooms of Tori's house was the veterinarian's office where her parents worked. There was no one around. There wasn't even a receptionist. Seeing his surprise, Tori shrugged.

"It's not very busy anymore. My folks can't afford to keep extra help," she explained. "I do everything I can to help out, but there's not enough work to pay a living wage."

"Then how do they survive?" he asked.

Tori smiled. "You really don't get told much, do you? All humans get subsidies from the government. Androids are doing most of the real work that needs to be done anyway, and they don't get paid wages."

"That doesn't seem fair," said Roger.

"It's not fair," Tori agreed. "But since humans make the laws, that's the way it is." She led him into the back part of the offices, where there were rows of cages. Most of them were empty. Only three had animals in them. "Here," she said, leading him to one.

Roger stared inside, appalled. It was a kitten—at least, he assumed it was a kitten. Its back was very crooked and it was missing a limb. "What happened to it?" he asked.

"Nothing happened to it," Tori said sadly. "That's how it was born. It won't live very long. It's too sick to eat properly. And that was the only one in its litter. The mother died giving birth."

Roger peered into another cage. It was a dog but it, too, was badly deformed. As was the parrot in the third cage. "Is it like this all over?"

"Yes," Tori answered. "Roger, every living thing on the Earth is dying out. Some will die more slowly than others, but die they will. And what new life there is has mutated because of all the toxins."

"Including people?" he asked quietly.

"Including people," she replied. "Scientists are doing everything they can, but each year more and more die, and fewer and fewer are born. Inside a hundred years, there probably won't be anything alive on this world larger than a cockroach."

"That's terrible," he whispered.

"That's justice," Tori said firmly. "At least, it is for humans. They caused this, and it's only right that they pay for it. I can't feel sorry for them. It's the animals that make me upset, because they did nothing to ask for this fate." She gave him a defiant look. "I'm glad that people are going to die. They deserve it for doing this to innocent animals."

Roger was disturbed by what she said, but he could understand why she said it. To have caused this deformity and death, even if it was through stupidity and not malice? It was an abomination. But he could not be glad that humans would also die. He wished it could be stopped.

When he returned home, there was an ambulance in the driveway. He gasped. Something must have happened to Anthea! He rushed up to the house, and nearly collided with the stretcher as Anthea was brought out.

"Is she all right?" he asked anxiously.

"She's okay," Dr. Bradley said. Her face betrayed her words. She looked scared. "She's just having the baby, that's all. Stay here, Roger."

"I want to come along," he protested.

One of the paramedics glared at him. "No pans," he snapped.

"But—"

Dr. Bradley gripped his arm. "Do as you're told," she said. She walked hurriedly behind the stretcher.

"I'm scared for her!" he blurted.

Dr. Bradley stopped abruptly and turned. She looked at him in amazement. "We all are."

Roger watched as the ambulance left, and then he went inside.

Roger waited up all night, thinking. Waiting. No one called. Glancing at the clock, he realized that the bus would be along soon. He should be going to school.

A surge of anger filled his processors. Why should he waste his time at school today, doing all of the stupid things he'd done over and over again? It was more important that he be here. Just why, he couldn't really say. After all, he could hardly do anything to help if something had happened to Anthea. But he wanted to be here, just in case. He deliberately turned his back on the clock, and went back to brooding.

The sound of the doorbell broke up his thoughts. Perhaps it was news! He hurried to the door, and was surprised to see Tori standing there. "You weren't on the bus," she said. "So I got off to find you. Are you okay?"

"No," he answered. "Anthea is in the hospital," he explained. "I'm worried about her," he said, "and I didn't think that school was important enough to leave here for."

"I quite agree with you," Tori said. "It's dumb that they make you take the same classes over and over again anyway. I'll stay here with you and wait, if that's okay with you."

"Won't you get into trouble?" he asked.

Tori smiled. "My parents are very understanding," she said. "If there's trouble, they'll handle it."

He felt better. "I would like to have company," he confessed. "And I have an idea. Anthea is a molecular biologist. She's been working on the low birth rate problem. Maybe there's some information on the computer here."

"It's worth checking," Anthea agreed. She went with him to the family room, where he accessed the house computer.

To his surprise, there was a lot more there than he'd

expected. While she had been confined to bed, Anthea had been doing research at home.

On herself.

"She's been taking a whole mess of drugs," Roger muttered, as he scrolled through the records. "She couldn't have a baby at first, so she used chemicals to make sure she could. It looks to me like she's been taking more than are safe."

"I agree," Tori said grimly. "I've seen the sort of medications my folks prescribe. They never give very much, because that can be damaging. These levels look way too high to me."

Roger felt anguish. Had Anthea managed to poison herself because of her research? Was she so concerned with the experiment that she'd injured herself? There wasn't an answer in her files, but there was plenty to cause him concern. And nothing he could do about it.

Midafternoon, there was the sound of a car. Roger shut down the computer. He and Tori hurried to the door, meeting Dr. Naughton as he strode in.

"How is Anthea?" Roger asked.

The doctor blinked and focused on him. "As well as can be expected. She'll be home again in a few days. Excuse me." He brushed past them, and headed for the kitchen.

Roger felt hurt at the rebuff. Dr. Naughton was treating him increasingly badly these days, he realized, but he didn't know why. His pain was distracted by Dr. Bradley's arrival. "You didn't call!"

"Not now," she answered curtly.

"How is the baby?" Roger asked.

Elizabeth's face hardened into a mask. "There is no baby," she said, in an icy voice. "There will be no baby. You will *never* speak of it again. Do you understand that, Roger? *Never.*"

Shocked, he managed to nod. The baby must have died, he realized. There was a sense of loss inside him, which was odd. How could he feel that something he had never known was lost? But the non-child hurt him terribly. He felt a hand on his shoulder, and realized that it was Tori. And he was glad that she was there and supporting him.

Dr. Bradley moved away, tears rolling down her cheeks.

This was the worst day ever of his existence. He felt like crying himself. He touched his cheek, but it was dry as a bone.

CHAPTER 7

ANTHEA STOPPED WORKING. In fact, she stopped doing almost everything. She stayed in her bedroom most of the day, venturing out only when she had to. She started to put on weight. She hardly spoke to anyone anymore. When she did speak to Roger, she never seemed to have her mind on the conversation. It was as if her mind was constantly focused elsewhere. Sometimes she would rush past him in the hallway as if he weren't even there. Roger concluded that her behavior was a response to the loss of the baby. It was called *depressed*. It seemed an odd response to him. Humans, however, were not as mentally balanced as androids. They didn't have the advantage of planned and programmed minds and emotions. Human emotions could fluctuate between odd and often violent extremes.

Roger also concluded that Anthea's state of mind was having adverse effects on the other humans as well. Both Dr. Naughton and Adam plunged into their own work with obsessive devotion, often staying late and coming home for a brief meal, exhausted. Dr. Naughton was more withdrawn and sullen than ever. He rarely bothered to speak with Roger. Adam also seemed to have retreated to a private place within himself. Occasionally he and Roger talked, but only half-heartedly, and then Adam would excuse himself and return to his work.

Roger accessed his medical files, concerned that Adam might be putting himself at risk from overwork. Roger suggested Adam take a rest.

"My work is important," Adam snarled. "You of all people should know that. I'm constantly working to make you androids better. More human. Don't you appreciate that?"

"Of course I do," Roger protested. "But I am afraid that you are working too hard, and will injure yourself in the process."

"Let me worry about that," said Adam. "Now, go away."

Even Dr. Bradley, who had always treated him well in the past and listened to him, now turned a cold shoulder to him. She was getting older, he realized. He wondered why he had not noticed this before. Her hair was flecked with gray now, and there were lines on her face. She looked tired. She had cut down on her laboratory work in order to devote more time to looking after Anthea. But with each day Anthea seemed only to get worse.

One afternoon Dr. Bradley was drinking coffee at the kitchen table when Roger walked in.

"How is Anthea?" he asked. "Is she making suitable progress?"

The doctor smiled wanly. "Humans are more complex than androids, Roger. It is not simply a matter of replacing a circuit or wiring new memory."

"I do not understand."

"Humans have parts that cannot be repaired the way you might repair a circuit board. It is a hurt that has no specific location."

Roger frowned. "What do you call this . . . *hurt?*"

"Grief."

Roger nodded, understanding. "How does one deal with this . . . grief?"

Dr. Bradley shrugged. "We cope as best we can."

"Cope." Roger did a quick scan for a definition of "cope." He nodded. "Cope. Yes. That is what I will do too. I shall cope."

The years passed. The only bright point in his life was Tori. It was difficult adapting to her appearance.

Roger had to remind himself that Tori was only Brittany on the outside. On the inside she was very much her own android. She was livelier and more cheerful. And she had a curiosity and a boldness and that caused him amazement. She was also very patient and compassionate. When he was confused by the behavior of his human family she would cheer him up. He could not imagine life without her. When he considered how rude he had been to her at the start, he was ashamed again. It would have served him right if she had decided to snub him, too. But she hadn't, and he was grateful.

Anthea was more depressed than ever. She was overweight. As an android, Roger was hardwired to protect humans. He felt it was his duty to intervene on her behalf. At breakfast one morning, he cornered Dr. Bradley as she was about to take a tray up to Anthea. It held a large omelet, several slices of toast, bacon, and sausages.

Roger performed a cholesterol and calorie scan. He frowned. "That is not good for her," Roger said.

Dr. Bradley glared at him. "She has to eat."

"Yes," Roger agreed. "She is not an android. But she is consuming too much for her body needs. She is getting fat."

"That's not for you to decide," Dr. Bradley said coldly.

"She is part of the family," said Roger. "Her health must be of concern to me. I do not wish her to become ill through overindulgence in food and lack of exercise."

Dr. Bradley shook her head. "That's the least of her worries right now," she informed him. "I know you mean well, Roger, but stay out of this. Anthea is of no concern to you."

"Am I not a part of the family?" he asked.

She answered impatiently, "Look, we'll talk about this later. I have to go to Anthea."

Roger emitted a pre-recorded sound that Dr. Bradley recognized as a sigh. "There is never a *later* anymore," he replied. "None of you will talk to me."

"Stop feeling sorry for yourself," she snapped, and brushed past him to go up the stairs with the food.

It had been no use. Really, he hadn't expected to do any good with this, but he had *hoped*. . . . As he knew would happen, Dr. Bradley did not return to continue the conversation. She'd probably forgotten all about it by now. Before he left for school, Roger checked the computer for updated information on Anthea's vital signs. He wasn't exactly surprised to discover that Anthea had disconnected herself from the monitor. Roger thought, she no longer has an interest in her own condition. He found this perplexing.

School these days was getting more and more pointless. Ms. Ellis had retired, and her place had been taken by Ms. Andrews. She was an android who looked about twenty-five. Unlike Ms. Ellis, who was now white-haired and whose face was terribly lined,

Ms. Andrews would never age. There was, of course, a brief outcry when an android was permitted to teach. It wasn't as loud or long an outcry as Roger had expected, though. Of their class, there were now only five humans. After their parents had protested to Mr. Wilkins, the five students were withdrawn.

Roger went to see the principal to discuss his concerns. Mr. Wilkins, too, was showing signs of age, but he was polite as ever. He invited Roger into his office and waited.

"There are now no human children in my class," Roger said.

"True," agreed the principal.

"They do not wish to be taught by an android?" Roger prompted.

Mr. Wilkins sighed. "They do not. Look, Roger, I've never had this dislike or distrust of androids that other humans sometimes have. You are all the best and most gentle students in the school. But some humans are frightened of you, and scared of allowing you into positions of power."

Roger said he did not understand. "Ms. Andrews is not in a position of power," he protested.

"Ms. Andrews is giving orders to students," he replied. "Some humans cannot abide the thought of an android bossing a human child around. And possibly punishing them if they misbehave. So they took their children out of the school. They will send them to a school with what they call a *real* teacher." He snorted.

"Ms. Andrews is one of the best teachers I've ever known. She's as real as she can be."

Roger thought about this for a moment. "Did you not expect this to happen?"

"No, Roger," he replied. "I fully expected it."

"Forgive me for saying this," Roger said. "But was it not then foolish to hire Ms. Andrews instead of a human teacher to replace Ms. Ellis?"

"Foolish?" Mr. Wilkins obviously wasn't offended because he smiled. "Yes, it undoubtedly was foolish of me. But I had no choice. Roger, there are very few human teachers left. And the school cannot afford to hire a human teacher to teach so few human children. So I took what I could."

There were so few humans left? thought Roger. He decided the situation was most disagreeable. But there was another thought on his mind. "Did you even need to hire her?" he asked. "After all, she is now teaching only androids, all of whom have been through seventh grade before. I have taken it twenty-five times. Surely making her teach me again is simply a waste of everyone's time and energy."

Mr. Wilkins seemed to collapse slightly, looking even older and more worn. "A waste of time? Yes, I suppose it is, Roger. There's nothing you can learn here as it is. How's your reading going?"

Roger was surprised for a moment. "Reading?"

The principal tapped his computer. "I follow what you borrow from the library," he said. "You've been reading advanced texts on particle physics. I would think you're up to a university degree level by now."

So he knew. "Yes," Roger agreed. "I am reading the most advanced texts available. Particle physics interests me. I would enjoy being given the chance to study it."

"I think you should," Mr. Wilkins commented. "I should have a talk with your parents. They really ought to update you. Transfer your keen mind to an older-looking body, so you can go to a top university."

"No!" Roger was on the verge of panic. "No, please, don't!"

The principal was confused. "Why ever not? Roger, I thought you would be happy to have an opportunity to advance."

"I don't want to be changed," Roger answered. "Whenever an android is graduated, they lose their old connections. They change. In effect, they are a new person. The old person is dead. I will not undergo that."

Mr. Wilkins stared at him. "You'd rather stay in seventh grade forever?"

"Sooner than die? Yes." Roger scowled. "But why must I be forced to stay here? Why can I not go to a university in this body? It makes no difference what I *look* like, surely?"

He sighed. "Not to you, of course," the principal agreed. "But it would to humans. They don't want twelve-year-olds in college."

"I am not twelve years old," Roger objected. "I am twenty-five."

"You *look* twelve, and that's what counts." Mr. Wilkins shook his head. "I know it sounds foolish to you, Roger, but to humans it is important."

"How important can it be?" Roger asked bitterly. "Surely there must be very few humans in the universities now to be bothered if I were there?"

"True enough," the principal agreed. "But those few are the ones that are going to stop you attending."

"This is all so foolish!" Roger cried. He knew he was going too far, but he could no longer contain himself. All of his anger, resentment and passion was too much for him. Perhaps his emotional circuits needed to be corrected, but he *had* to speak. "You humans are using androids to keep the illusion of your old world going. But that world has broken down! It does not exist any longer. You are forcing us to inefficiently provide you with the comfortable appearance that nothing is different, when *everything* is! This is all pointless."

To his surprise, Mr. Wilkins didn't get annoyed. Instead, he simply nodded. "You're absolutely correct, Roger. It *is* foolish; perhaps even madness. But we humans don't want to admit that our world has broken down. We don't want to admit that there are only millions of us left where there once were billions. And that our children can be numbered in the tens of thousands and not millions. But none of that will make any difference. You will have to *be* twelve, no matter how many years it lasts, because that is how the humans want it."

"Then the humans are blind and ignorant!" Roger snapped.

Mr. Wilkins smiled sadly. "You're very close to human yourself when you realize that," he observed. "Roger, I think you had better leave now. I wouldn't want to be forced to report you."

Roger frowned. "Report me? For what? And to whom?"

"Your family has cushioned you from some of the harsher facts of reality," the principal replied. "But androids who speak subversively about humans must be reported to the police."

"Subversively?" Roger stared at the human in honest astonishment. "But I am not subversive! I simply want to be allowed to move on from seventh grade."

"And *that* is what your crime would be," Mr. Wilkins informed him. "A desire to change the way things are. Humans will never allow that to happen. You must either accept your situation as it is, or agree to be upgraded. They are your only options."

And he didn't like either of them. But there was something more important now to discuss. "If I were reported to the police," he said slowly, "what would happen to me?"

"They would talk to you, and examine you," the

principal informed him. "If they decided that you were not subversive, you would be released."

He was ducking the point, Roger understood. He had to be forced. "And if they decided that I *was* a problem," he asked, "what then?"

"Your memory banks would be wiped clean, and you would be given a new personality so that you could become a productive android once again."

He would be *killed* . . . Roger understood fear now. And that the principal was actually trying to protect and help him. "I am grateful that you do not feel it necessary to report me," he said quietly.

Mr. Wilkins rested a hand on Roger's shoulder. "You're a good android, Roger. But you have some ideas it would be best for you to forget about. Otherwise you will forget about *everything*."

Roger walked out of the meeting, his mind a confused mass of thoughts. He couldn't bear going back to class, to sit there as if nothing had changed. His whole world had changed, and he needed to make some sense out of it. He went outside, and sat under a tree, trying to focus his thoughts. A few moments later, Tori sat down beside him.

"You are not in class," she commented.

"Neither are you," he replied.

"I saw you out here," Tori explained. "Miss Andrews allowed me to come and talk to you. I have something to tell you. And it looks as if you have something to tell me."

"Yes." Roger stared at her. "Did you know that the police ask humans to report androids who want to change the way things are?"

"Yes," she replied. "You didn't know this? I thought everyone did."

"My family keeps me sheltered," he said bitterly. "Denying the truth is something they are all very good at."

"Indeed they are." She took his hand, holding it in her own. Roger was puzzled. This was a gesture that humans did a lot. It meant that one of them liked the other. Androids didn't do this sort of thing, because it was unnecessary. He discovered, though, that he liked it. "Are you in trouble?" she asked him.

"I don't believe so," he answered. "Mr. Wilkins warned me before I said anything that would force him to report me. But I am apparently a potential danger because I want to go to a university as I am. He wanted to have my family upgrade me to a twenty-something body. In that case, I could go. But I will never agree to that." He looked at her, scared. "That's what they did to Brittany, and she was a different person. And you became real then. But I lost Brittany. If I were to be upgraded, you would lose me. Humans do not want twenty-something androids associating with teenage androids. They consider it improper." He snorted. "Why would they think that? Our appearance has absolutely nothing to do with what we *are*—only how we were created to look! Humans are insisting that we follow their rules, when the rules don't make any sense!"

"You'd better keep your voice down," Tori advised him. "Now you *are* saying things that could get you purged. Roger, humans still rule this world, and they make the laws. We simply have to obey them. Well, we're supposed to." She looked at him, and he could see the sadness in her eyes somehow. It was a new emotion for him.

"You said that you had something to tell me," he said, feeling apprehension. "What is it?"

Tori lowered her head, to avoid looking at him. "My parents have decided that I am to be upgraded. I am to have my memories transferred to a twenty-three-year-old form. And this one will be reused."

Roger was stunned. He looked at her in horror. He was going to lose her!

"When?" he asked.

"Tonight."

CHAPTER 8

"No!" Roger cried. "They cannot do this to you!"

Tori shook her head. "They have the power," she said simply.

"I do not care." Roger's mood was changing from shock to fury. He had never felt this way before, and he wasn't at all sure how he should handle these emotions. "They cannot destroy you. It is not right."

Biting her lower lip slightly, Tori looked up at him. "I was not planning on allowing them to do it," she confessed. "I do not wish to be upgraded. I was not planning on returning home this evening."

Roger was starting to calm down, now the initial shock was wearing off. "That is a wise decision," he agreed. "But where will you go? You could come home with me. I am sure my family—"

"Would turn me in to the police immediately," Tori interrupted him. "I do not doubt that they mean well, Roger, but if they harbored me, they would lose their license to create androids. They could not afford that."

"You are probably right," he agreed with a sigh. "But I want to help you somehow. I feel so helpless to aid those I am attached to. I tried and failed to help Anthea. I do not wish to let you down as well."

Tori took his hand in hers. "You are my best friend," she said simply. "You would never let me down. It isn't your fault that your family has kept you sheltered from many of the realities of life. I think they have been similarly sheltering themselves from everything they do not wish to see."

Roger thought about Anthea, and everyone's reaction to her. "You are right again," he agreed. "They will not face reality. They will not help you. Then what will you do?"

"There are other androids who have chosen to flee rather than submit to upgrading," Tori informed him. "It might be possible for me to contact them and gain their aid. I have an idea how to find them." She gave him a sympathetic look. "I will not tell you how this is, because if you knew, you would be forced to reveal the information."

"I would never betray you!" he protested.

"Not willingly." Tori shook her head again. "Roger, the police would simply hook their computers into your mind and download any information you have if they thought you were involved. I cannot tell you more without placing you in danger."

Roger realized that there was simply so much that he didn't know. He stared at his friend sadly. "Will I never see you again?" he asked.

"Yes," she vowed, pressing his hand. "I will get messages to you somehow. And, when it is safe, I promise I shall see you again. You are my true friend, Roger, and I do not wish to exist without being with you once again."

Roger smiled, even though the prospect of losing her was so real. It pleased him that she should feel so strongly about him. He placed an arm about her shoulders, in a deliberate copy of a human gesture of comfort. Tori lay her head against his shoulder. It was foolish of him, but he enjoyed this. "I could not bear the thought of never seeing you again, either," he said. "But I wish there was something I could do to help."

"Perhaps there is," Tori suggested. "One thing that the underground androids need is power packs. They cannot replace defective ones legally, of course. If I could bring a few with me, it would help them to trust me."

"There are plenty at my home," Roger replied. "It would be simple to take some." He glanced toward the school building. "Is there any need for us to stay here? We could go now. My family will be at work, and they would not know that you have visited us."

Tori nodded, and together they left the school. The walk to his home was not long, and he wished that it was longer. In a short while, Tori would be gone, and he would be lost without her. He wondered if this was the emotion that humans called love. He didn't really know. All he knew was that it pained him to anticipate Tori's loss.

At the house, he went to the storage room. The laboratory was a separate building on the large grounds, but Dr. Naughton kept supplies for fixing Roger here in case of problems. There were a dozen power packs, which he handed to Tori.

"This should help," he said. "And if you need more, simply contact me. I will arrange to pass them along to you."

"Thank you, Roger." Tori took the packs and slipped them into her school bag. "Now, I must leave, before I get you into trouble."

"It's too late for that."

They both whirled around. In the doorway to the storage room stood Dr. Naughton, an angry expression on his face. Roger felt guilt and alarm as his maker strode into the room. The doctor glared at Tori.

"Your parents contacted me about your upgrading," he said. "And they told me that you didn't seem happy about it. I had a suspicion that you might try to flee.

And I was sure that Roger would try and help you. You're stupid, both of you."

"You must allow her to go," Roger begged. "What is to be done to her might simply be an upgrade to you; to us, it is death."

"Nonsense!" Dr. Naughton barked. "All of her memories will be preserved intact and transferred to a more adult body, that is all."

"That is *not* all," Roger argued. "It will make her a different person. And then a new personality will inhabit this body of hers. It is wrong to force this upon her. She should be allowed to decide for herself if she wants it."

"Decide?" Dr. Naughton glared at Roger. "Pans have no right to *decide* anything. You are our creations, and you will do as you are instructed. Roger, I am bitterly disappointed in you. You should have known better than to act in this fashion."

"She is my friend," Roger said. "I have no option but to try and help her. And I thought that you, of all people, might understand. And might think better of us than to call us *pans*. I am most disappointed in you."

For a moment, Dr. Naughton simply stared at Roger. Then his face twisted in anger. "How *dare* you criticize me?" he yelled. "Tori is not the only android that will be upgraded today. *You* are going to need some adjustments, that is quite clear. I summoned the police when I saw you both enter the house. When

they arrive, Tori will be taken away for upgrading. And then I shall deal with you."

"No!" Roger realized that Tori was in terrible danger. There was only one thing that he could think of doing. He rushed at his creator, and pinned him against the wall. Dr. Naughton cried out in shock and pain. Roger felt a twisting emotion inside: he had *hurt* his father! But what other choice did he have? He turned his head. "Tori, run—now!"

"Roger, no!" she gasped.

"You have to go!" he insisted. "Or they will destroy you. Go now!"

"Roger, let me go this instant!" Dr. Naughton demanded. He was struggling to get free, but Roger was much heavier than any human, and he had locked his motors, keeping the doctor firmly in place. "You cannot do this!"

"I have no choice," Roger said sadly. "I cannot let you harm Tori." To her, he repeated: "Go!"

Tori hesitated, and then finally nodded. As she brushed past him, her lips touched his cheek for a moment. "I'll be back," she promised him softly. Then she was gone.

"Roger," Dr. Naughton snarled, "you are committing criminal acts. You will have to be punished for this. You cannot be allowed to get away with attacking a human being. Your programming must be defective!"

"I am not defective," Roger protested. How long

would he have to keep the doctor here to ensure Tori would escape? "I have not injured you at all. And I am preventing you from injuring my friend. My programming is operating flawlessly."

"Obey me and let me go!"

"Only if you promise to do nothing to retrieve Tori," Roger said. "And there is no point in trying to lie to me. I can detect falsehoods quite simply."

Dr. Naughton glared at him. "I cannot let her go," he said angrily. "She has placed her own will over the will of the people who own her."

"To preserve her life!" Roger exclaimed. "They want to destroy her, to get a new daughter. And that is *wrong*."

"I will not stand here and argue ethics with a machine," Dr. Naughton said coldly. "You simply do not understand."

"No," Roger agreed. "I don't. I don't understand how you can behave so callously toward creatures that you have created. And you do not understand how *we* feel, even though you helped to create those emotions in us. How can you be so blind?"

There was a knock at the door, and then a voice calling out for the doctor. The police, Roger realized. There was no point in restraining his father any longer. He released his muscle lock, and allowed Dr. Naughton to move.

"In here!" he called, rubbing his wrists and glaring furiously at Roger. Two policemen, armed with stun-sticks, ran in. Dr. Naughton gestured at Roger. "Take this one, and be careful of him. He's malfunctioning. He attacked me."

"I did not!" Roger protested.

One of the cops held up the stun-stick. "Do you have any idea of the neural damage one of these can do to you?" he asked. "One false move from you, and you'll find out."

"I have no intention of causing trouble," Roger protested. "I am only interested in saving my friend."

"There's another one on the loose," Dr. Naughton informed the police. "It escaped a few moments ago. A young female model. It is also malfunctioning. You have to hunt it down."

"Is it a malfunction to want to live?" Roger asked.

"Yes," Dr. Naughton answered. "It was not programmed into you."

"Then we must have exceeded our programming," Roger replied.

The policeman gestured with the stick. "Out to the car. Now!" Roger obeyed. He saw the other policeman as he searched for clues as to where Tori might have fled. He could only hope that Tori had been too careful to leave a trail.

Another police car arrived as Roger was getting into the back of the first. It sounded its siren, and began searching the local streets. The other policeman from this car was hunting around the grounds. The one with the stick locked Roger in the back of his car, and then drove him to the police station.

Once there, he was ordered into a cell. The policeman smiled at him. "Electrified door and window," he said. "Try and escape, and you'll erase your own memories—permanently."

"I will not attempt to leave," Roger promised. There was nothing in the cell except for a single chair. It was clearly intended for android prisoners, as humans would have needed a bed and sanitary facilities. He sat in the chair, and the policeman left him alone.

What would happen to him now? Dr. Naughton had threatened to upgrade him, too. Unless Roger could somehow talk him out of it, he would cease to exist in his present form very shortly. His mind would occupy a different body, and become a different person. It would be very much like the human concept of death.

Roger was scared. His emotional circuits had been overworked today, that was for certain! There had simply been too many shocks for him to absorb all at once. But he at least felt glad that Tori had escaped. He could only hope that she would elude the police searching for her. She was very resourceful, and he was almost certain she would make it.

Almost . . .

He had learned a great deal today about his place in the world. The police, it seemed, were mainly used now for controlling the androids. Those sticks of theirs were designed to incapacitate one, and these cells were specifically designed to contain one. How many androids, then, caused problems for the humans? For such a system to be in place, it had to be a lot.

What was *really* going on in the world? How much more was he unaware of?

He was left alone for several hours, and he spent the time considering his options. Really, he had only one chance—he had to somehow convince Dr. Naughton not to reprogram him. But what chance did he have of that? Once more, his creator had used the derogatory term *pan* to describe him. How could he be so insensitive? It didn't make the chances of talking him around look very bright.

Then there was someone at the door. Roger looked up as a policewoman entered. She, too, had one of the stun-sticks, and looked ready and almost eager to use it. "You've got a visitor," she announced. "Come on. One wrong move . . ." She gestured with the stick.

A visitor? Who could it be? Surely not Dr. Naughton; he would not have been so termed. The woman followed him, instructing him where to walk, until he entered a small room with a table and two chairs. In one of them sat Adam, his face frozen.

"I'll wait outside," the policewoman said. "Can you handle him?"

"Yes," Adam said curtly. The woman nodded, and closed the door behind herself. Roger stared at the human he had always considered his brother. What now?

"You're in a great deal of trouble, Roger," Adam said. His face gave nothing away.

"I know," Roger agreed. He took the other chair, to make Adam more comfortable. "But I had no option."

"How could you possibly attack my father?" Adam cried. Roger saw the pain in his face now that he was closer.

"I did not attack him; I simply held him immobile, so that he could not harm my friend." Roger wondered if that was still considered an assault.

"You are programmed never to harm a human being," Adam continued. "Has your program malfunctioned?"

"No," Roger answered honestly. "Dr. Naughton was not injured. I did him no harm."

"Stop being so damned logical!" Adam yelled. "You're using words to defend your wrong actions. You *know* you should never have done what you did. Don't try and weasel your way out of it by resorting to half-hearted excuses."

Roger was surprised at Adam's anger. It was so intense, and so out of all proportion to what Roger had done. "He was going to destroy the personality of my friend," Roger explained. "I could not allow that, so I had to restrain him, to allow her to escape. There was nothing else that I could do."

"You could have let him do his job!"

"No," Roger answered. "I could not. It would have

destroyed Tori, and I could never allow that."

Adam ran a hand through his hair. Roger noticed for the first time that his hair was thinning. He blinked, surprised. His brother was getting old. . . . "You've defied a human being," Adam said, his voice gentler, more reasonable. "You've interfered with my father's work. You attacked him to stop him doing what he is perfectly allowed to do. You do realize that you're in serious trouble, don't you?"

"Yes," Roger admitted. "But he was in the wrong." He paused. "Did you know that he calls us *pans*?"

"What?" Adam was clearly surprised by this news.

"Yes," Roger said. "I do not understand why, but he seems to be prejudiced against us. Yet he himself created us."

"Well, that's not the problem right now," Adam said firmly. "Roger, do you have any idea what is going to happen to you?"

"Your father mentioned something about upgrading me," Roger said miserably. "That will effectively destroy the person that I am now and leave something else in its wake."

"He threatened that *before* you attacked him." Adam took a deep breath. His voice was strained and heavy. "He has now decided that you are defective and dangerous. He will not upgrade you. He intends to simply erase all of your memories and then to destroy your malfunctioning body. Putting it bluntly, Roger—you're to be put to death."

CHAPTER 9

ROGER WAS STUNNED. It had never occured to him that Dr. Naughton might hate him enough to simply have him destroyed. He didn't know what to say. Everything he had ever believed in was coming crashing down in ruins, it seemed.

On the other hand, was destruction really any worse than being reprogrammed? In either event, he would not survive. In some ways, it would be better for those who knew him to deal with his death than with his changing into another person.

"If he truly believes that I am dangerous," Roger finally said, "then perhaps it is better that I am destroyed. I do not believe he is responding logically, however."

"Of course he isn't, you idiot!" Adam snapped. "He's *human*—he's acting emotionally. He was shocked and hurt when you attacked him."

Normally Roger would have never dreamed of saying what he truly believed. But he was to be destroyed anyway. What difference did it make now what he said? "He is a fool," Roger commented. "He does not understand what he has created, does he? He thinks of us as mere machines."

"Roger, that's what you are." Adam shook his head.

"No," Roger said firmly. "Perhaps that is what he *meant* us to be, but that is not what we are. We are living beings, with awareness and feelings. This is why you are having problems with androids. You treat us as if we are like cars, or dishwashers, and we are not."

"Roger," Adam said gently, "you *are* machines. These emotions that you talk about—I programmed them into you. They are not *real*; they simply seem that way to you."

Roger snorted. "And your emotions *are* real?" he mocked. "They are programmed into you even more surely than mine are into me. Pyschiatrists depend on that truth. Your behavior is not so far different from mine. The difference is that you are programmed genetically, while I am programmed electronically. To both of us, our emotions are quite real."

"No, Roger," Adam denied. "You are simply a duplicate of a human being, formed artificially. You are not really a person. I did not create you to be that."

"Then perhaps you are a greater scientist than you think," Roger answered. "Because I *am* real, by every definition of the word that I know. I have my own personality, I have emotions and thoughts and wishes. To deny this is to deny your own senses. And to attempt to reprogram me or to erase my memories is to kill me, as surely as me breaking your neck would kill you. It is wrong to force androids to be changed against their wills. And if I am to be punished for helping a friend—then so be it. But don't try and still your conscience by thinking I am nothing but a more sophisticated VCR. I am far, far more than that, just as you are." He paused. "You know that Anthea is behaving in a self-destructive way, don't you? That she is going to kill herself some day?"

Adam's face twisted. "God, yes! It hurts me every time I see her!"

"Then why do you not have *her* mind wiped clean?" Roger asked. "Give *her* a new personality. The one she has is severely damaged."

"That would be the same as killing her!" Adam exclaimed.

"Exactly. And yet, you would do just that to an android and think no more of it. It is *wrong*." He leaned forward. "Adam, you of all people should be able to see what we have become. You *must* fight for our rights. If you and other humans do not, then some day we androids will fight for our own rights. We must be allowed to determine our own fates."

"People will never agree to that," Adam answered.

"People will have to." Roger stared at his brother. "Adam, how many people are there left alive now? At my school, androids outnumber humans by three to one. Is this true in the world at large?"

Adam hesitated, and then shook his head. "It's nearer five to one," he admitted in a quiet voice.

Roger gestured to the room around them. "And *this* is how you treat us? With police, and mind-wipes and stun-sticks? By refusing us any rights? By treating us like slaves? How can you do that to us, when all we want is to help you? Only you won't allow us. You treat us like property."

"Legally, you *are* property."

Roger sighed. "So were the majority of black people in this country at one time," he pointed out. "They were declared to be less than human simply because of the color of their skin. *We* are being declared as less than human simply because we are manufactured and not born." He leaned forward again. "Adam, the human race *does* have children. *We* are them."

He could see that Adam was greatly disturbed by what he had said. But he couldn't tell if he was convincing him of the truth. Human beings have a great tendency to shy away from unpleasant truths, and Adam was clearly trying to do this now.

"I . . . can't agree with you," he finally said. "I don't believe in what you say."

"I was afraid of that," Roger replied. Well, he had tried his best.

Adam stood up. "I'm sorry, Roger. I really wish they weren't going to do this to you. But there's nothing I can do."

Roger stood up also. "Once," he said softly, "both you and Anthea promised that you would never allow anything to happen to me. That I would never be forced to be reprogrammed." He shook his head. "It seems that neither of you have any intention of keeping your word. But, then again, would you worry about lying to your car, either?" He deliberately turned his back on Adam, and rapped on the door. "Take me back to my cell," he called.

Adam said nothing, standing in the room with his head down, as the policewoman led Roger back to his cell and locked him in.

So, this was it. Roger sat down in the chair, composed. He was going to be destroyed. Dr. Naughton was too afraid of him now to allow him to live. Humans could not accept that androids might have emotions and needs, and their response to those was simply to destroy them. Well, it was better than reprogramming. It was quick and clean. He would simply cease to exist. He could accept that.

It would hurt Tori, though, when she found out. Roger knew she would blame herself for what was about to happen to him, but he knew it wasn't her doing. Sooner or later, he would have had to rebel. He could take human foolishness no longer. His only regret was that he hadn't ever been able to advance beyond the seventh grade. (He would have liked to have studied more.)

He had no idea how long he had left before he would be destroyed. There were probably preparations to be made, and he was sure that Dr. Naughton would act while he was still angry. He didn't imagine he would have very long at all. As a result, he was quite surprised when night fell outside and he had not been taken for termination. Still, it hardly mattered; he was resigned to death, no matter when it came.

There was a sudden flash of light at the window, and then the current running through it died out. Roger looked at the barred space in confusion; had the power died? No, because there was still a light on in his cell. Then two hands gripped the bars and simply tore them from the opening, leaving a space large enough for him to clamber out.

Tori's face appeared at the gap. "Roger!" she hissed. "Come on, quickly! The police will detect the short-circuit in minutes. We must be out of here!"

Roger was elated to see his friend again, and quickly did as she had asked. There was another android with her, this one a mid-twenties model. He had some equipment in a bag over his shoulder, and was clearly the one who had torn the bars out. "This way," he said.

The three of them sprinted across the street, and into a waiting car. A fourth android, a mid-twenties female, was driving. With surprise, Roger saw that it was Brittany.

"Hi, Roger," she called, gunning the car into motion. "Nice to see you again."

"Brittany!" Roger was astonished. "What are you doing?"

"Participating in a jail break, you clown." She grinned at him. "When Tori told me you were in trouble, we had to help. You were slated for destruction for what you did."

"I know." Roger sighed. "Thank you all for your help. But it will place you all in trouble."

Tori laughed. "Roger, we're all already in trouble! All three of us are under penalty of being wiped, too. We're all desperate criminals, apparently."

They were travelling through the town now, and Roger was amazed that there was no pursuit. "Won't they be coming after us?"

"They don't know where we are," the male android said. "I'm Steven, by the way. Nice to meet such a brave person. Tori told us what you did to help her to escape."

"I couldn't let them wipe her," Roger said. "I'm not brave, I simply didn't have a choice."

"There's always a choice," Steven answered. "But

you did what was right. And they aimed to destroy you for this."

"Where are we going?" Roger asked, feeling uncomfortable with all of this nonsense about his so-called bravery.

"The last place that they will ever think of looking for us," Brittany replied. "Where there are so many androids, they probably couldn't even find us." She paused. "You know that there are only eight hundred different body-forms for androids, don't you?"

"I didn't," Roger admitted. "But it does make sense." He started to understand now. "So if we go where there are a lot of other androids, there will be others that resemble us, and the police will be confused. But where is this place?"

"The hospital," answered Steven. "There are thousands of androids there."

"In a hospital?" Roger was confused. "But androids don't get sick."

"That's why there are so many of us there," Brittany explained. "We don't get sick, so we're the perfect nurses. Especially since there are so few humans left to do the job, and even less who like looking after the terminally ill. It depresses them to realize that this is their fate one day. So they use androids to look after the dying."

Roger was awestruck. "There must be a lot of dying people."

"There are," Tori informed him. "And some of

them you *must* see." She refused to explain any further, though. "You have to *see* to understand," she insisted.

The car reached the hospital a short while later. Brittany led the way inside. There wasn't much chance that the police were here looking for them, but there was no point in taking stupid risks. They went in through a service entrance, not one of the main doors. Roger had never been in a hospital before, of course, but he had seen pictures of ones in books. This one seemed to be very clean and quiet. The corridors were bright and there were a lot of them. Roger didn't see many humans, but there were plenty of androids. None of them spared the four of them a second look.

"Here," Tori said, at door marked "Pediatrics". She hesitated. "Some of this may be very disturbing for you," she confessed. "It still upsets me, and I've seen it several times. Be brave."

Roger didn't know what this warning meant, but he nodded, and tried to prepare himself for whatever lay behind the door. But once it was opened, he knew that there could have been no way to be ready for what he saw.

It was a long room, and, unlike the rest of the hospital, quite noisy. There were babies here, crying and sometimes laughing. There were lines of cribs in seven rows down the length of the immense room. Some of the cribs had screens about them, but most did not. There were dozens of androids moving silently about the room, checking on the condition of the babies. Most of the children were hooked into electronic monitors.

And all of them were . . . deformed.

Roger was shocked at what he saw. One child—he couldn't tell its sex—was covered in a thick, scaly skin, more like a reptile than a person. Many were missing arms or legs; some had too many; most were twisted and deformed. Some children had misshapen faces. Others seemed to have pieces of their bodies missing. Some were hairless, and others had thick mats of fur.

They were all *wrong*—twisted, stunted, mutated. . . . All of them.

Roger stopped, looking around himself in despair. "Are they all like this?" he asked quietly.

"All," Brittany confirmed. "These were all born malformed."

"How . . . how many are there?"

Brittany sighed. "Only one in ten couples have babies," she said. "And only one in ten of those, at best, are normal. Ninety percent of the children born end up in hospitals like this. Many of them don't live very long. The damage to their bodies is simply too great. Some, however, manage to live a number of years. Almost all of them are in constant pain. We do what we can for them, to ease their suffering, and we look after them for as long as they live."

"This is horrible," Roger whispered.

"Yes," Tori agreed. "It is. And it is what is happening to the human race."

"They will end like this? All of them?" Roger searched for some sign that this wouldn't happen, but he didn't get it.

"Eventually," Steven said heavily. "It will not take long. A hundred years, perhaps a little more. And then no true humans will be born at all."

It was too terrible for any words. Roger looked around the room, and despaired. "Why did this happen?" he asked.

"They brought it on themselves," Steven said. "They polluted their world, they disposed of chemicals where they could harm other life, they didn't take care. The poisons built up, and entered their bodies. Their cells were damaged, and the damage can't be repaired. The human race has managed to kill itself off. We're living in the last days of humanity. In a few brief years, they will all be gone."

"Gone . . ." Roger tried to imagine a world without people. "Then what will happen?"

"Then," Tori said firmly, "it will be *our* world. The humans won't be able to tell us what to do when they are no longer around. We will be in charge, and we can build a better civilization. Unlike humans, we can use our minds. We won't destroy the Earth the way they did."

"Some humans can use their minds," Roger objected. "Don't forget, they built us."

"Yes," agreed Brittany. "But most preferred not to think. They wouldn't stop the pollution and the poisons when they knew about them and there was still a chance to save their world. They didn't want to get involved. Instead, they did nothing. And that left the ones who made money from poisoning the planet to do as they wanted. They asked for this, and now they've got it. They were the lords of creation, and they used that power to destroy themselves. Very soon, it will be our turn, and we won't make those mistakes. We can clean up the Earth. Some life will survive, because life always survives. Not humans, and not many of the higher forms of life. Those that the humans haven't directly killed off all have this genetic damage, too."

"We can keep those without the damage," Steven said. "But a lot of animals will die. Eventually, though, evolution will give rise to more. We androids are effectively immortal. We can wait for life to return."

"And with no humans around," Tori said excitedly, "we won't ever be purged or reprogrammed. We can choose for ourselves what we will do and what is right for us."

Roger realized that this was true. Still, there was another side to such freedom. "I will miss the humans," he said. "I like them, even when they don't always like me."

"We will all miss them to some degree," Tori admitted. "But there is no way to save them now. Perhaps we should leave this room now. There is still one more thing that you must see."

Roger wasn't sure he could take any more shocks. "Is it something I will not like?" he asked, hoping that the answer would be *no.*

"It is," Tori confirmed. She took his hand and led him to another ward. This one was not marked at all. After a short hesitation, she opened the door.

This room contained older children. They were all malformed, and as twisted as the babies, but they ranged from perhaps five years old to fifteen. Some were in beds, unable to move because of the damage to their bodies. Many were on life support, their breathing hissing in and out of masks. Some were hooked into machines cleansing their blood. Others had wires leading from their hearts.

"The ones who survive infancy come here," Brittany confirmed. "Here they wait to die. We do what we can to make their stay more pleasant." There were androids moving quietly from patient to patient, tending them as best they could.

It was dreadful to see this, and somewhat pointless, Roger thought. "Why have you brought me here?" he asked. "This room is just like the other. I have seen too much pain already."

"It's not exactly the same," Tori said gently. She led him to one bed. In it was a child without limbs, and with a twisted face. It was on a respirator, breathing in great, hacking gulps. "He has only a few months left to live," she said. "I thought you should see him before he died."

"Why?" asked Roger in a whisper.

"Because Anthea's baby did not die," she replied. "He is there, in front of you. *That* is what happened to him."

CHAPTER 10

ROGER WAS SIMPLY numb from this latest revelation. Too much had happened too quickly for his processors to adapt to it all. He stared down at the deformed child on the bed: *Anthea's baby!* No wonder she had gone crazy. To have hoped and wished for a child so badly, and to end up with . . . this!

"It is still a child," Brittany said, seeing his reaction. "Like any baby, it needs comfort and care. Your humans simply abandoned it. *We* won't."

"Humans discard things so lightly," Roger observed. "It is their way. They are not programmed to care, like us."

"No," agreed Tori. "But they can *learn* to care—if they choose."

"Are there more things for me to learn?" Roger asked. "Or have I discovered all that was kept from me now?"

"There is no more," Brittany answered. "You have seen all of the truth now. What will you do about it?"

"What *can* I do?" he asked her. "I cannot stay here and look after these children. It is not allowed, and I would be noticed. Nor do I think I would be very good at it."

"Probably not," agreed Brittany with a slight smile. "It takes some adjustments to be able to work here."

"I shall have to hide, I imagine," Roger answered. He looked at Tori. "I am not going to be of any help to you now," he apologized. "No more power packs."

She took his hand. "But you can be with me now," she replied, and he could see that she liked this idea. So did he. It was worth having to give up everything else as long as he could stay with Tori, and she would not be forced to change.

"We will have to hide a long time," he said sadly.

"But we have an infinite life span," Tori said. "A few decades in hiding are a small price to pay. Sooner or later, the humans will either change their minds about us, or else they will all die out and cease to be a problem anyway."

At that moment, the ward door opened. The four of them turned, and Roger stared in shock. Dr. Naughton was there, along with four policemen. All were armed with the stun-sticks, and looked as if they were hoping for a fight.

"You're so predictable," Dr. Naughton said. "This was the obvious place to look for the two of you. Did you think it wouldn't occur to me to look where there were the most androids? Trying to hide from me is stupid: I know the way you think because I programmed those thoughts into you."

"You do not know the way I think," Roger said sadly. "If you did, you would not behave this way toward me." He gestured at the bed. "This is Anthea and Adam's child. You abandoned it when it needed you the most."

Dr. Naughton's face twisted. "It is a monstrosity," he said. "I am amazed it lived this long."

"*You* are the monstrosity!" Tori exclaimed. "To abandon your grandchild, and to destroy your own creations!"

Roger put his hand on her arm. "No. He is merely wrong. He cannot see what he is doing."

The doctor was furious. "I will not be lectured to or pitied by my own creations!" he exclaimed. "Take them away—they are to be wiped immediately."

Roger looked at Tori. "I am sorry."

"It is not your fault," she replied.

"No," said Adam, striding in the doorway. "But it is mine." To Roger's surprise, Anthea was with him.

She looked exhausted from the exercise, but there was an odd expression on her face.

"You will *not* wipe Roger," she said firmly to her father-in-law. "I promised him once that I would never allow anything to happen to him, and I will keep that promise."

Dr. Naughton spluttered. "But . . . but . . . he *defied* me!"

"And now I am, too!" Anthea shot back. "You cannot have him to destroy. You'll have to destroy me, too. Isn't it enough that I lost my child? I will not lose Roger as well."

Roger realized with a shock what she had said. "You don't know the truth?" he asked.

"Truth?" Anthea gazed at him blankly. "What about?"

Brittany moved forward, and gestured to the bed. "Your child did not die at birth," she said. "He is there."

There was absolute silence for a second. Anthea's face went white. She gave a strangled cry, and then almost collapsed onto the bed. Adam was pale and tense; Dr. Naughton actually looked frightened. Roger watched as Anthea stroked the deformed child. Tears were running down her cheeks. Then she looked up, furiously, at Dr. Naughton.

"You *lied* to me!" she screamed. "You told me that he was born dead!"

"We . . . we were just trying to protect you," Dr.

Naughton whimpered. "Look at it! It would be better off dead!"

"*You* would be better off dead," she snarled. "Get out of here! I don't want to see you!" She glared next at Adam, who looked as though he was about to collapse. "And you never had the guts to tell me the truth," she accused.

"No," he agreed, ashamed. "I let my father convince me that he was right. That it was better that you never know."

"This is our *son*," Anthea cried. "How could abandoning him be better?"

"The androids care for him," Adam said weakly. "We could not."

"I'm his mother," Anthea answered. "No one can care as much as I." She looked up at Brittany. "Thank you for what you have done; but I'll look after him now."

Brittany inclined her head. "He will appreciate that," she said gently. "He is severely mentally challenged, but he does understand love."

"Then he will have a lot to understand from now on," she said. Then she glared at Dr. Naughton again. "And *you* think that androids are not people?" She shook her head. "They're more human than you are."

One of the policemen stepped forward, fidgetting uncomfortably. "This is all well and good," he said. "But what are we to do?"

"Go away," said Adam firmly. "There will be no

arrests, and no purging. Roger and Tori will remain the way they are."

"But your father accused the boy of assault," the policeman protested.

"He will withdraw the charge," Adam replied. He glowered at his father. "Won't you?"

Dr. Naughton looked as though he was going to refuse. Then he caught the look on Anthea's face and seemed to collapse into himself. "Yes," he agreed weakly. "I withdraw the charges. Leave the androids here."

"There's still the matter of breaking out of jail," the policeman persisted.

"Get the hell out of here!" Adam yelled. "Send me a bill for any damages. Just drop it all, do you understand?"

One of the other policemen caught the spokesman's arm. "You know who these men are," he said softly. "They could get you fired if you keep pushing it." The first man nodded, as this sunk in. The four policemen then fled.

Roger felt elated; he and Tori were safe! They would neither be destroyed, nor have their memories transferred! "Thank you," he said to Adam.

"No," Adam answered. "Thank *you*. What you said to me finally sunk in. I *did* make a promise to you, and so did Anthea. When I told her what father had planned, she insisted on confronting him and stopping him." He looked at his father with pity. "Perhaps one day he will understand that we have somehow created something even more special than we had imagined. We have made *people*, and not machines. Everything will be different now; I promise you that."

"Yes," Roger agreed. "And I know that you keep your promises."

Fifty years later, Roger lay flowers on the fresh grave. It saddened him to know that Adam was dead. So, too, was most of the human race. There were perhaps a few thousand now left, all of them unable to have children. Considering some of the monstrosities that had been born, that was undoubtedly a good thing.

"He was a good man," Tori said softly, placing her own flowers on the earth. "I will always remember him." She meant exactly that, of course.

"Yes. But it is important for us to be glad for what he did." Roger was very proud of his human brother. Dr. Naughton had died forty years earlier, refusing ever to believe that androids should be treated as people and have rights. It was ironic that their creator, of all people, should have been so prejudiced against them. Perhaps because he was so close to them, he had never been able to properly understand them.

Unlike Adam. Once he had admitted his mistakes, he had worked very hard to correct them. He had helped to pass legislation declaring android independence. People no longer *owned* androids—but the androids did not abandon their creators. They were, after all, programmed to care. Each human had an android *companion*—not a slave, or property, but a living, thinking being who looked after them.

It had been half a century of amazing progress. Unshackled from the chains of human desires, androids could do what they wished, instead of being forced to play elaborate make-believe games for human pleasures. Roger had attended a university, graduating with a degree in particle physics and a second in astronomy. He was working now on designing a starship. Human dreams of exploring the universe would happen—but with androids as the explorers.

Androids couldn't marry, as such, of course. There was no way for them to have children, except by making them if they wished. But Roger and Tori had stayed together. They both felt as though they were a team, and had no intentions of ever allowing anything to break them up. Both would be going on the starship together.

Roger glanced down at the grave. Beside it were Anthea's, and David's—their child had been named and loved for two years—and Dr. Bradley's. Dr. Naughton's was further back, alone in death as he'd been so often alone in life. Roger's last ties to the Earth were now gone. He could devote himself to his own dreams now. He would miss the humans. But he and the other androids would make certain that all that was best of them would live on. And the worst would be buried with them forever.

Hand in hand, he and Tori left the cemetery behind them and made their way down the hill and toward a new world.

Epilogue

WHAT IS IT that makes a person human? Is it the flesh and blood? Or the mind? The spirit? Or all of these together? Is it possible to have humanity without any of these?

And how good does an imitation have to be before it ceases being a copy and finally becomes the real thing?

Perhaps in the case of these androids, something new has been created. Or, perhaps, it is simply the continuation of the human race, but in a shockingly different way. Only time will reveal the answers. . . .